THE SEARCH FOR GRISSI

A winner!

MARY FRANCIS SHURA has written over twenty books for young people. Born in Kansas, not far from Dodge City, the author has lived in many parts of the United States, including California and Massachusetts, but currently makes her home in the western suburbs of Chicago, in the village of Willowbrook. The mother of four grown children, Mary Francis Shura enjoys tennis, chess, reading, and cooking—especially making bread.

TED LEWIN, an author in his own right, has illustrated many books for children and is well known for his fine-arts work. He lives in a brownstone in Brooklyn with his wife, Betsy, also an author and artist, and two rescued stray cats, Bones and Dundee. It was Dundee that posed for Grissi.

THE SEARCH FOR GRISSI

MARY FRANCIS SHURA

Illustrated by Ted Lewin

AN AVON CAMELOT BOOK

AVON BOOKS
A division of
The Hearst Corporation
1790 Broadway
New York, New York 10019

The Dodd, Mead edition contains the following Library of Congress Cataloging in
Publication Data:

Shura, Mary Francis.
  The search for Grissi.

  Summary: Eleven-year-old Peter feels uncomfortable at home and school after
his family moves to Brooklyn, until his search for his sister's missing cat opens up a
new life for him.

  1. Children's stories, American. [1. Cats—Fiction. 2. Brooklyn (New
York, N.Y.)—Fiction. 3. Schools—Fiction] I. Lewin, Ted, ill. II. Title.
PZ7.S55983Sb   1985   [Fic]   84-28624

First Camelot Printing: March 1987

Printed in the U.S.A.

OPM   10 9 8 7 6 5 4 3 2 1

With love and gratitude to
ROSEMARY
who led me there

Contents

THE
SEARCH
FOR
GRISSI

1

DeeDee

The next-to-the-worst thing that can happen to an eleven-year-old boy in a strange school in a new city is to have to walk his little sister home from school every day. The absolutely worst thing is to have that sister be DeeDee Gregory.

I speak from the pain of experience. I'm Peter Gregory, and DeeDee is my sister. She is skinny, seven, and spooky. She's the kind of kid who disappears if you blink. She can disappear all by herself, but since she is also the kind of kid who draws other kids as if they were flies, she has even learned to make a whole bunch of other skinny, spooky little girls disappear with her.

In fact, the whole business with the gray cat called Grissi began because I blinked and turned the corner at the same time. But that didn't happen until the second day of school.

To tell the truth, I had really dreaded those first few

days in our new school. I wished we'd had more time to settle into brownstone Brooklyn before having to start. All my favorite things were still sitting in boxes in my room on the fourth floor of that tall house.

And Mom had enrolled us in a private school. DeeDee and I had always gone to public school back in Peoria. I'd been afraid that a private school would be different and, from the beginning, my worst predictions came true.

The very first day, the Monday after Thanksgiving, started off with my new teacher having me stand up in front of the class to be introduced. I really felt self-conscious with that whole roomful of strangers staring at me as if I were extraterrestrial. Only when Mr. Lazarus announced that I was from Peoria did those sixth-graders show any life. Some of them looked at each other with their eyelids half closed, as if they were passing a joke around under their lashes.

"Peoria Pete," someone whispered, starting a wave of shoulder-shaking, silent giggles all around the room.

I really hate name-calling and having labels like that stuck on me. A long time before, I'd had trouble with teasing back in Peoria. Then it had been because some kids felt that drawing and painting were things a real guy didn't do. I'd gotten that all behind me, back home, and I had already planned not to go through it again.

That first day whenever Mr. Lazarus asked a question that I thought I could answer, I put up my hand like everybody else did. Sometimes my answers were right and sometimes they weren't. Since that's the way I have always been at school, I figured I might as well start out here the same way.

But I kept having the feeling that the other kids were staring at me. They never met my eyes at all when I glanced around at them, so maybe I imagined that they were watching me when I was looking the other way.

Since nobody came to sit down by me at noon, I ate lunch by myself.

When school was dismissed that afternoon, I walked out by myself, while the rest of the class walked off in little groups. That was all right with me. I wasn't really hot on anyone's seeing me take on my baby-sitting chore with DeeDee and the inevitable cluster of little squealers she always acquires.

Then I realized that one of the guys hadn't left. This curly-headed kid still stood there, looking at me with a kind of serious expression on his face. He was a lot bigger than I am. When bigger kids show interest in you like that, you have to watch out. Sometimes they are just looking for a chance to prove how much bigger they are, and I'm not a fighter.

"Peoria," the kid said, after a minute. "I don't know anything about Peoria." His voice was different—flat, as if he were keeping any expression out of it.

Since that didn't sound very threatening, I smiled at him. "I don't know much about Brooklyn, either," I admitted.

"A bunch of the kids and I sometimes have a Coke after school, just around the corner. Want to come along?" Then he added, "My name is Colin Cramar."

Something kind of jumped inside me. Maybe I would have friends here after all. I liked the level way he looked at me, even though he was really so sober faced.

Then I remembered. In the first place, I couldn't go anywhere but home because I had to lead DeeDee there by the map Mom had drawn for us. In the second place, if he hung around until she got out, he would discover that I was a glorified baby-sitter.

"Thanks a lot," I said. "Maybe some other time." I might have sounded brusque without meaning to, because I wanted to go with him so bad and couldn't.

He looked at me thoughtfully, then nodded and turned away. "See you around," he said in a final kind of way.

I felt rotten, watching him walk away, but what could I do? It was bad enough to be known as Peoria Pete, without having a nursemaid label stuck on top of that.

When you are moving to a new place, you worry about a lot of things, like making friends and staying out of trouble and not being made fun of. A lot of good it would do me to keep my painting and artwork a secret if they were going to tease me about everything else.

My attempt to keep Colin Cramar from seeing me baby-sitting DeeDee and her new friends turned out to be a wasted effort. When I had herded those little girls to within a block of our house, I saw Colin Cramar again. He was walking down the street by the church near our brown-stone. He was still wearing the loaded backpack he'd worn at school so I figured he hadn't been home yet, either.

DeeDee and her new friends aren't exactly loud, but they are shrill. They were playing some skipping game that sent them into gales of giggles about every half a block. Colin turned at the sound, looked at them, and then me. He didn't say anything or even nod at me. He just turned off down the little street that ran by the church.

My second day at school was pretty much like the first one. By the time the final bell sounded, I still hadn't made a single friend there, nor had I figured out what my teacher, Mr. Lazarus, expected of me. But I told myself it was just a matter of our getting used to each other.

Maybe I should have predicted what was going to happen when I walked outside that door. I was still on the steps when I saw this bunch of four guys standing on the sidewalk, looking back at me and laughing.

"Hey, Peoria Pete," one of them yelled. "Have a good time playing nursemaid, Peoria Pete."

Naturally all the other kids turned around and stared. Then that bunch of guys practically killed themselves, slapping their knees and guffawing.

I could feel myself getting red from embarrassment. I could feel myself getting mad, too. I hadn't done anything to any of those guys and here they were, going out of their way to make fun of me over things I couldn't help.

I was still just standing there trying to figure out what to do about it when DeeDee came dancing down the steps with two of her new friends. One of the girls was a blonde with thick braids and a square, serene face. The other was dark like DeeDee, except that her hair was a short, springy mop of curls that fell in her face every time she moved. The contrast between what a good time they were having and the way I felt made me stamp off down the street.

DeeDee and friends didn't pay any attention to me as we started toward home. I returned the favor.

I could hear those guys still calling after me and shouting with laughter. The madder I am, the faster I walk. Since I was pretty mad, I was probably half a block ahead of DeeDee and her little clones when I turned the corner.

If I hadn't been so upset, I would have remembered the way home from having walked it the day before. As it was, I wasn't sure. I stopped just a second and took the map out of my pocket to check it. When I saw we were right on course, I stepped back around the corner to see what was keeping the little girls from catching up.

They were gone.

I yelled for DeeDee. Some people walking by glared at me, but I didn't hear her voice. None of the shops along the street looked like anything that would interest little kids. I ran back down the block anyway, looking in all the windows. Men's clothing, insurance, a Middle Eastern restaurant that smelled fantastic, then an alley.

There they were, all three of them, standing with their

heads together like a miniature football team in a huddle. They were standing so close together that I didn't realize DeeDee was holding something.

"All right for you, DeeDee," I said, relief wobbling my legs.

She looked up and ran toward me, carrying this gray cat in her arms. "Look what I got, Peter. Look what I got. Isn't he beautiful?"

He was beautiful. One thing about that cat, he was beautiful. He was darker than most gray cats, dark like charcoal when you smudge it with your finger to make shadows in a drawing. His face was broad and friendly looking, and his eyes were the clearest, brightest yellow I had ever seen. In a flash I knew which color I would use from my paint box to produce that tone just one shade darker than lemon.

I nodded. "He's great but put him down."

"He's her very own cat now," one of the kids piped up. "That man gave him to DeeDee to keep."

I looked around. There wasn't any man in the alley. There was only a line of green trash cans, that cluster of little girls, and a pair of pigeons with green and purple chests hobbling along on a ledge way up and complaining in that hollow, throaty way that they do.

"Put him down," I repeated. "You can't just take a cat because someone gives it to you."

"But he's my cat," DeeDee explained. "The minute Captain saw me with him, he nodded and said this was my cat."

"Captain," I scoffed. "Who is this captain who gets to say that you can have some old stray cat? That's something for Mom and Dad to decide."

"He's not a really stray cat," DeeDee protested. "Captain said he wouldn't let me pick him up except he knew this cat lived with people some time."

"Then let him go back to those other people," I told her. "You can't have a cat without permission."

I could almost see my words flying right over the three heads.

"His name is Grissi," the blonde girl said in a dreamy way. "Isn't Grissi a beautiful name?"

"DeeDee's really lucky," the one with the mop of dark curls said wistfully. "My mom won't let me have an animal."

"Neither will DeeDee's," I told them. I reached over to take the cat from her. Instead, DeeDee danced away from me and ran toward the street, with her two little friends right behind her.

"At least I get to ask," she called back at me.

The sidewalk was crowded with people hurrying along both ways. I had this instant vision of losing that kid again, this time with cat.

I shrugged. Let Mom break the news to her that she couldn't just come home with a cat this way. At least I had tried.

I had to run a little to catch up with them but, believe me, I didn't let them out of my sight again.

2
Grissi

Now you have to realize that this Grissi wasn't any kitten but a full-grown cat. Later, at home, Dad weighed him on the bathroom scale and he came in at fifteen pounds. DeeDee's arms had to be aching by the time we made it all the way home, but she didn't complain. The blonde girl with the braids who had told me the cat's name had to turn off before we reached our house. The other girl walked on past, turning to look back and wave a couple of times before Mom came to answer our doorbell.

That house has two front entrances. The door to the ground level is in behind a little iron gate that encloses a tiny front yard. The second entrance is fancier. It is a huge double door at the top of a high brownstone stoop and opens into the front hall of what Mom calls the "parlor" floor. With Mom still unpacking, I hadn't any idea where she would be. I ran up the stoop and took a chance on the big front door. I was lucky because Mom was close enough to come right away.

DeeDee will never see the day that she is as pretty as Mom. Mom is well rounded where DeeDee is straight up and down. Even with a scarf tied around her head and a smudge of dirt on her cheek, Mom looked great. The way her smile tightened into annoyance when she saw us was not that great.

"Look, Mama," DeeDee said quickly. "This is my cat, Grissi. Isn't he beautiful?"

Mom's mouth opened and then shut again without any sound coming out. Before I could tell her that I had tried to keep DeeDee from bringing the cat home, she said quietly, "Congratulations, Peter."

"I told her she couldn't have it," I protested.

Mom looked at me thoughtfully, then shrugged. In fairness, she has lost enough rounds to DeeDee herself to give me the benefit of the doubt.

"But he's my cat," DeeDee wailed. "He was given to me for my very own."

Mom shook her head. "Now listen to me, DeeDee," she began. "You know in your heart that Peter is right. Put the cat down and come inside."

"But, Mama," DeeDee wailed. "I'm lonesome here. Can't we just wait and see what Daddy says? If I put him down and he goes away, I might never ever see him again."

Don't think those words didn't come back to haunt me later.

People say I am talented just because I can draw anything I am looking at. DeeDee's talents are a lot more useful in just the day-to-day management of a life. For instance, she can make tears come and fill up only the bottom half of her eyes and just hang there in pools until she gets her way. That little seven year old can pull Mom and Dad's strings as if they were puppets and they don't even know they're dancing.

The moment Mom hesitated, she was lost. DeeDee leaned over and set the cat down right on the marble doorstep. Grissi looked up at Mom, took two graceful steps into the front hall, and arched his back to rub against her leg. Then, with a glance at DeeDee as if to ask if she were following, Grissi walked into our house as if he had lived there all his life.

When Mom sighed and shut the door after us, I figured that DeeDee was rounding second base and was on her way home.

By the time I finished my cookies and milk, DeeDee had a plastic mat down on the floor for that cat. Grissi, hunched in front of a blue bowl, was lapping milk as I started up to my room.

I counted the steps as I climbed. Those stairs don't have proper landings but just hug the wall most of the way and then curve around at the top of each flight. There were fifteen steps going straight up from the parlor floor and five more to make the bend. From that third floor up to my room there are ten straight steps and four around. I was only counting steps to distract myself. I get really disgusted when other people feel sorry for themselves, yet there I was, about to drown in my own self-pity.

But it didn't seem fair. DeeDee already had two skinny friends and was more than halfway to a cat.

All I had was a big room full of boxes to unpack and a whole sixth grade full of kids laughing at me.

One of the worst things about feeling sorry for yourself is that you keep thinking of "ifs."

If Dad hadn't accepted his promotion, we would never have had to tear our whole world apart like this.

If Mom had put her foot down, Dad would probably not have taken the new job. After all, Mom'd had the most successful interior decorating studio in Peoria. Instead, she had said, "If I can make it in Peoria, I can make it in Brooklyn."

If we had moved during the summer instead of in November, I would have started with other new kids and wouldn't be so conspicuous.

If. If. If.

If only a few things were like they had been back in Peoria. Take this house we had just moved into.

Our house back in Peoria was big and old with noisy plumbing, but it had a wide front porch and was set back from the street with enough side yard to play baseball in.

This brownstone was ridiculous. It was in a row of houses that all looked a lot alike. None of them had side windows except for the two at the ends.

I told you about that front door going into the bottom

23

floor. That is where the kitchen would be in a normal house. Instead, there is a whole separate little apartment down in that basement. Mom said it would be perfect for her interior decorating business, but it made all the rest of the house strange.

Who ever heard of having the kitchen upstairs? A kitchen is what you walk into when you come in the back door. Bedrooms were supposed to be above that, with the attic up on top where you put old things that don't matter any more.

In this house, the kitchen and dining room are on the parlor floor, at the back. Then on the next floor up is the big master bedroom and another room where Dad has his desk and books. DeeDee's room and mine are at the very top, on the fourth floor. Looking down, the backyard seems so far below that if I were bothered by heights I would be having a nosebleed.

Not that it was much of a backyard anyway—just a path, some bushes, a pair of pale white trees, and a bench near the back. A little alley runs through our block behind the gardens. Mom says that is unusual. She thinks a farmer's lane ran along there a very long time ago before Brooklyn was a big city or even a town.

Instead of unpacking my boxes, I stared out the window. All the gardens were the same size but it was amazing how different they managed to be. The people on one side had made a fancy little garden with a walk winding around a birdbath. Lumpy white ghostlike shapes lined the walks. Mom guessed those were rose bushes being protected from winter. The yard on the other side was really formal, with huge white rocks half covered by evergreen plants. Maybe that garden just looked oriental to me because I had seen Mrs. Joon, who lived there. She is even shorter than Mom and has a wonderful, glowing face with shining dark eyes. The family beyond that, at the end, has a big, dark dog that hurls himself furiously against the fence and barks whenever anyone passes down the alley or the side street.

Now, I like to draw better than almost anything in the world. What I like to do is to look at something until I see the shape that is hidden inside it. Almost everything fits into a few shapes when you do that. One of the trees in the rose garden was a fir tree shaped like a cone upside down. That would be fun to draw.

I was still leaning on the windowsill looking out when Mom called from downstairs.

DeeDee was waiting at the kitchen door. "Mama wants you to walk down to the store with me," she said.

Mom was too embarrassed to look back at me. Instead she fumbled in her purse while she talked.

"We need some cat food," she said. "Just a few cans."

Did I say halfway home? That cat was at third base and still running. It was easy to see how Grissi had managed to get this trip going. He was sitting hunched up beside that milk saucer with his paws tucked under his chest. His expression of patience would have made a statue of Buddha look restless.

I knew that sooner or later Mom would let DeeDee

wander around alone. At this rate, later was going to seem a long time coming. A street of shops was only a block away. I had been in every one of them the first day we came. I was hoping to get a little job like the one I'd had back home in Peoria. I swept out Mr. Foster's grocery store there, and unpacked boxes and sometimes delivered things on my bike. It was neat to have the money and that separate little world of my own. None of the shopkeepers here even wanted to consider how handy I could be.

At the front door, DeeDee said, "Just a minute, just a minute," in an urgent way. Then she ran up all those stairs to her room, which was just next to mine. She was back quickly with her red wallet bulging out of the pocket of her jeans.

"Mom gave me money," I told her.

She nodded and skipped down the steps ahead of me.

The church on the corner takes up most of the block. Someday I am going to sit somewhere and draw it. It has practically every kind of shape on it somewhere. Mostly it is a lot of brick rectangles set together, but a little courtyard like an empty cube is set into one end. Above the round window, way up high, rises a spire like a skinny, squared-off cone. Even in winter, noisy little birds chattered in the ivy that clung to its sides. Someone was playing the organ when DeeDee and I walked by.

I thought I caught a glimpse of Colin Cramar off down that little street but I sure didn't stop to look. That Colin had to be a real tattletale. Nobody else had seen me baby-sitting DeeDee and her friends. He *had* to have told those guys who made that big fuss in front of school. All I needed was for him to see—and report to the other kids—that I apparently never stepped out on a street without a skinny little girl hopping along beside me.

A book shop called The Corner Shelf is next to the church, with a drugstore just beyond. In front of the grocery, rows of boxes were tilted to show off the bright colors of the fruit. DeeDee popped in there and I followed.

The grocer, whose name was Anthony Pucci, hadn't been very friendly to me when I asked for a job. He grinned now from ear to ear when DeeDee ran up to him.

"I have a cat," she told him. "A gray cat named Grissi."

"A cat," he repeated and winked at his wife. Mrs. Pucci turned from the shelf she was stocking and smiled at DeeDee.

"How nice for you," she said. Then she nodded. "And for the cat. Then it's cat food you need."

DeeDee followed her to the right shelf and brought back all the little cans of cat food that she could hold with both arms. "Look what tiny cans they are," she told me hastily. "Grissi is a big healthy cat." She set them on the counter and raced off again.

Mr. Pucci was giving me Mom's change and putting the cans into a bag. I heard DeeDee chattering to Mrs. Pucci at the back of the store but I didn't pay any attention. Just as I took the grocery bag, DeeDee came up swinging a wicker basket with a yellow calico cushion in it.

"Where did that come from?" Mr. Pucci asked his wife.

"She needed something for her cat to sleep in," Mrs. Pucci told him. "I had it out back. I can always get another one. The price is still on it."

DeeDee set the basket on the counter and took out her wallet. "I have enough," she told me defensively, spilling out folded dollars and a heap of change.

"But DeeDee," I protested. "That's your birthday money and all your savings. You don't even know what Dad is going to say about keeping that cat when he comes home."

Those tears began swimming in DeeDee's eyes again, and Mrs. Pucci was glaring at me as if I were a half-grown ogre.

I just gave up. I should quit fighting that kid and sign up for lessons from her.

I could see through her like a pane of glass. Dad might not really want a cat around the house. But he could hardly make DeeDee give up Grissi after she had spent her entire fortune on him. Dad was no more an ogre than I am the son of one.

The basket was so bulky that I carried it home for DeeDee. We had a cat named Grissi and that was all there was to that.

3

Hal Sanders

I guess I was pretty stupid not to figure out I had a fight coming at that new school. When you have made it through eleven years without getting your knuckles bloodied, you forget that some people operate on a more basic level. My best friend back in Peoria was named Tim. He and I had had some shoving contests through the years. They usually ended up in an hour or so of frozen silence that warmed up by itself. There's a lot of difference between shoving someone around and smashing your fist hard in somebody's face.

It was the Friday of the week that Grissi came. I had just finished my fifth day in the new school and, although I didn't like it much better than I had the first day, I at least knew I was going to survive.

I walked out the front door just as usual to wait for DeeDee and Company to join me. Colin wasn't anywhere around. I had watched for him since that first day. I didn't want to fight him, but I did want to let him know that I didn't appreciate his poking his nose in my business. If he hadn't gone and told everybody about my baby-sitting DeeDee and her friends, all the name-calling would never have begun.

By Friday I learned who those four guys were who had waited out in front to jeer at me. Their ringleader was a boy named Hal Sanders. He laughed first and loudest when someone gave a wrong answer in class. He did petty, mean things like following people down the hall, making silent fun of them by mimicking their walks. Even though he was the smallest of those four boys, the rest followed his lead. Maybe they were afraid of his laugh. The sound of it made my teeth tingle like biting down on aluminum foil.

I saw the four of them gathered over by the curb but didn't bother about them. In fact, I was watching the front door when I realized they were singing all together in a high-pitched, nasal way. What they were singing made me swing around to stare at them. I knew the tune from somewhere. They had it just wrong enough that I couldn't pin it down. The words were plain enough: "Ain't he sweet, Our Peoria Pete, walking his little baby dolls up and down the street?"

Some of the other kids had stopped to watch them mince along with their hands raised and their shoulders bouncing up and down against their ears. The other kids looked at them and then at me. But give them credit, nobody laughed or cheered them on.

I was just stunned enough not to have moved when DeeDee appeared at the top of the steps. DeeDee is famous at our house for being a quick study. You never have to repeat anything to that kid. She's been known to answer questions before you finish them.

DeeDee's eyes went round, and her mouth tightened into a straight line just the way Mom's does when she is really angry. She didn't give those guys time for a second verse. She threw her book satchel behind her and shot down the stairs on those skinny little legs.

I could have told Hal about those legs. She showed him. In less than an instant she was all over him, beating him with her fists and kicking his shins so fast and hard that he was too busy trying to defend himself to get hold of her. But he kept screaming and finally caught her by the arm. He's as big as I am and DeeDee weighs nothing. He caught her and threw her away from him like something worthless. Luckily she staggered backward against another guy, who caught and held her, still kicking and flailing, at arm's length.

Maybe I had just never been mad enough to fight before. In that moment, I understood what it meant to see red. I charged blindly down those stairs and went for Hal. He was still hopping and yelling when I grabbed him by the shoulder. I pinned him against a car that was parked at the curb and let him have it right in the face with my balled-up right fist.

I felt the hot stickiness of his bloodied nose even as I

was grabbed from behind and pulled away. I was trying to shake off whoever had me by the back when I realized how quiet it was all of a sudden. The other guys were sort of stiffened into frozen poses.

I looked around straight into Mr. Lazarus' face.

"That'll do, Gregory," he said in a quiet, no contest voice. "I want all five of you inside."

"He hit me," Hal started yelling. "You saw him do it. He just hit me."

"Inside," Mr. Lazarus repeated, his voice only a shade louder.

"We didn't do anything," one of Hal's friends put in.

"The next fellow that pipes up gets his punishment doubled," Mr. Lazarus said. Then he turned to DeeDee.

"Are you waiting for your brother?"

"Yes, sir." Her face was still splotched with anger and streaked from tears.

He glanced at her two little friends. "The library is open, Trudy and Nell," he told them. "You three girls wait there for Peter."

I could see DeeDee choking on what she wanted to say, but she and her friends marched back into the building as quietly as the five of us boys did.

To my astonishment, Mr. Lazarus made me wait in the front of the classroom alone while he led Hal and his friends off to a little alcove at the back that he uses as an office. I have never lived through a longer five minutes in my life. There was no telling what those guys would say to him. Who would he believe? After all, they could have gone to that school for years for all I knew. I was a new kid. What did Mr. Lazarus know about me?

I'm no different from anyone else. I sat there trying to figure out what he was going to say and how I was going to answer him to make myself look good. When he finally called me in, he sat behind his desk, very relaxed. He spun a pencil between his thumb and index finger, his expression so jovial that it confused me.

"I want to congratulate you on the aiming of your fist," he said. "Two inches lower would have destroyed several thousand dollars worth of orthodontia. Expensive injuries like that get a lot of attention from parents. A bloodied nose is considered something that goes with the territory of growing up a boy."

He didn't ask me how the fight started. He didn't ask what made me hit Hal. In fact, for a minute, I felt as though I was back in class and he was giving a regular lecture the way he did on history or science.

"An effective human being," he said, "is one who manages to survive and function efficiently in any environment in which he finds himself. People are part of any social environment. When you come as a stranger, you walk on other people's territory and batter their egos without even knowing it. But violence has to be the last resort of a thinking animal." He stopped and looked up at me quizzically.

"Any comment?" he asked.

What I was really thinking sounded so simple and stupid after all those big careful statements that I couldn't answer him.

"Go on," he urged. "What are you thinking?"

"He hit my kid sister," I blurted out. "And I lost it."

He nodded and rose to walk back and forth with his hands in his pockets.

"But why?" he asked. "Aren't you going to tell me what made that little second grader come flying off the steps like a hawk for the kill?"

I shook my head, smiling at his simile in spite of myself. Then I realized. "You must have seen the whole thing," I told him.

He nodded. "I was warned. I got there for the whole show."

"Warned?"

He nodded. "You may be the only one who didn't see it coming. That tells me fighting isn't your usual game. I appreciated your friend's warning me."

I stared at him. Friend? He went on just as if he could read my mind.

"I won't give you his name, but you must have other questions?"

My head was working on about three levels. I was relaxing inside. It didn't sound as if I would be kicked out of school or something final like that. At the same time, I was thinking how much I liked this man. The question on the third level was what I asked.

"What did I do to start all this?"

He sat down and leaned back, smiling at me. "Any society, like this class for instance, has a delicate balance. When a new member is introduced, everything shifts a little bit. The new person gets attention that used to go to someone else. Sometimes established members of the group resent this, particularly if the newcomer shows some really admirable trait, like volunteering answers in class right away."

I stared at him. "But a lot of my answers are wrong."

He chuckled quietly. "That's not the point. The other kids give wrong answers, too. The point is that you took the risk of making a fool of yourself in a new, strange situation. That takes daring. Very self-conscious people resent that kind of courage."

I stared at him a long minute without realizing I was doing it. It didn't bother me to be wrong in class. Why did it bother me so much to be kidded about other things?

"Something more?" he asked, prodding me.

I shook my head. "I'm really sorry about the fight," I told him. "I never thought I'd hit anyone like that. But DeeDee . . ."

He rose, came around his desk, and put his arm around my shoulders. "Just be glad she struck the first blow. Being beaten up by a second grader isn't going to be a story that Hal, or any other sixth grader, is apt to tell at home."

I grinned. "Being defended by one isn't going to be anything to brag about either," I reminded him.

"I'm glad that's your problem instead of mine. Just cut

a wide berth, Peter. When the newness wears off, you'll find yourself."

DeeDee and her friends had apparently talked the fight over and forgotten it. The minute I appeared at the library door, they were on their feet, putting on jackets to go.

Two things nagged at me all the way home. How could I have a friend and not know it? What in the world had Mr. Lazarus meant about my finding myself?

I also wondered what to do at home about that fight. Should I tell the story my own way or take a chance on how it would come from DeeDee?

I expected DeeDee to run straight to Mom the minute we were in the door, but she didn't. Instead, she called Grissi and made a little clucking sound that he seemed to recognize. He came flying down the stairs, his tail stiff with welcome. He lay draped around her neck like a fur scarf while we had our snack after school. Mom fixed herself a cup of coffee and sat down with us. She made us both laugh at her description of how she'd played hide-and-seek with Grissi while she organized the coat closet. In just those few days, Grissi had taken over center stage with all of us.

I worked most of that afternoon on my homework. When you like a teacher, you want to do better work. DeeDee interrupted me once to come down to see what Grissi was doing. It was pretty funny all right. He had figured out how to get into one of Mom's kitchen drawers from the back. He was lying in there all flat on the placemats, with just his eyes peeking out.

"Now watch," DeeDee told me. She pushed the drawer tight shut and we waited a minute.

Very slowly, Grissi pushed the drawer back open, to look up at us again with those clear yellow eyes. What a great cat.

Because Dad was home on time that night, we all had dinner together at the big round table in the kitchen. Mom had originally put a row of little herb plants on the shelf along the windowsill, but they had ended up in the dining room because Grissi claimed that shelf for his own. He curled up and lay there, rumbling with pleasure, as we ate.

Mom was really bubbling with how she would get her decorating studio ready to go right after Christmas. Dad had met another man from Illinois in the New York office of his firm. Over lunch together they had talked about the Chicago Cubs. I was scooping ice cream for the cake Mom was slicing when Dad suddenly looked over at me.

"Your mom and I have been hogging the conversation all through dinner. What happened in the lives of the Gregory kids today?"

DeeDee glanced at me and then away. "Our teacher finished the book she was reading and we start a new one Monday," she told him.

I had to laugh. I was all prepared to listen to a kid's-eye view of that fight and she didn't even mention it. "I had a long talk with Mr. Lazarus after school," I told Dad. "He's really a great guy. I can't wait for you to meet him."

"That's good to hear," Dad said, looking at me a little quizzically. He knows I'm not a kid to hang around and talk to teachers after class.

"I was in there because I got into a fight and bloodied a guy's nose," I explained. "I was lucky not to mess up his teeth. But thanks to some nameless friend and DeeDee, I got through it in one piece."

With that much out, it was easy to tell the rest. I thought Dad was going to split when DeeDee left her dessert to get up and dance around, showing him how she had lit into Hal.

Mom clearly didn't think the story was all that funny. She caught her lip between her teeth with a look of concern. "I hope you won't have any more trouble from this," she worried aloud.

"I plan to keep the kid around for protection," I told her, nodding toward DeeDee.

Getting to sleep that night was slow.

From my bed back in Peoria, I could see right into the heart of a big mulberry tree that Dad threatened to cut down every year when its berries got ripe. Flies came from everywhere for those mulberries and, for about two weeks, our shoes left blue stains on Mom's carpets.

39

From my bed here, I saw the glow of the city only gradually darkening into the night sky really high up. Dad said I would be able to see the Statue of Liberty from there if some hospital buildings weren't between it and me. When I put my pillow at the foot of my bed, I could see the tops of the World Trade Center, with an aerial and a red light sticking up from one of the big rectangles.

For the first time I noticed how the lights from the side street cast shadows of crossed wires on the blank wall of my room. I had meant to hang some posters there, but maybe I wouldn't. I liked the mysterious way that etched design kept changing with passing cars, just when I thought I had it figured out.

But the real mystery was who had warned Mr. Lazarus about the fight. I decided that whoever it was had wanted his name kept secret for fear of being called a stoolie or a tattletale. Nursemaid Peoria Pete could sympathize with that, all right.

4
Butch

On a calendar, Thanksgiving and Christmas look all crammed up together. When you are plodding through those four weeks, though, they stretch themselves out into the longest month of the entire year.

All that weekend after my fight with Hal, I dreaded Monday when I would have to go back to school. If it hadn't been for that crazy cat, Grissi, I couldn't have stood it. But this was Grissi's first weekend at our house. Having all of us at home clearly delighted him.

DeeDee, who loved Saturday morning cartoons, thought Grissi should sit beside her to watch them. Always genial, he stayed where she put him only until her attention strayed. Then off he went, to check up on the rest of his people.

Since our house is old, some of the doors are hard to shut really tight. I heard Dad talking to someone when I passed the master bedroom and figured it was Mom. When

I found her in the kitchen, I kidded her that Dad had taken up talking to himself. She laughed and said he might as well for all the good it was doing.

"It's that Grissi," she told me. "When your father went into the bathroom to shave, the cat nudged the door open and followed. Dad put him out a few times and then gave up. He even cleared the shampoo off that shelf by the tub for Grissi to have a place to sit. I expect them both down any minute."

I thought Grissi would just follow Dad down. I had underestimated that cat. Dad came in, wearing his Saturday clothes, with Grissi riding on his shoulder.

"That's my cat, you know," DeeDee told him, coming in just behind them.

"Tell *him* that." Dad laughed. "And you might also tell him that unwinding an entire roll of toilet tissue is beneath his dignity."

Mom turned to stare at Dad. "You are kidding?" she said hopefully.

"I wadded it all back up," Dad said. "He had a wonderful time doing it. We can have those doors fixed so he can't open them."

Grissi sat on the window ledge, rumbling his pleasure, while we all had breakfast.

But Grissi was fair. He raced up and down the stairs with DeeDee until she dropped with exhaustion. He spent a long time dreaming in my window while I made some sketches of him. And when I looked for Mom about five o'clock, she was making lists at her desk downstairs with Grissi taking up half of her rolling chair.

The Monday I was dreading finally came and I went back to school. Strangely, nothing happened there. It was almost as if I had become invisible through body contact with Hal. Even his friends quit seeing me. When they glanced my way, their eyes would slide over me as if I were greased. That was fine with me, but I caught myself studying the faces of the other kids, wondering who had warned Mr. Lazarus.

I thought about Colin Cramar a lot. Not that I thought he was the one who had acted as my friend but because he was an interesting kid and I kept seeing him around our neighborhood.

He had that kind of square head with a blocky jaw that I always put on knights in armor when I draw them. He never smiled the way most kids do, but his expression wasn't cross at all, or unhappy. In fact, even without smiling, he managed to look genial and friendly. He didn't seem to have any special friends. But although he didn't hang around with anyone, everyone seemed to like him.

Pretty soon I learned the names of the other kids in my class. It was amazing how many had the same names as my old friends back home. There were two Matts, and both a Stephen and a Steve. I was the only Peter, but there was a Tim. The girls' names ran to things like Mindy and Janie and Dana. One girl who reminded me a little of

DeeDee was named Siobhan, which I was afraid to pronounce after I saw it spelled.

But knowing people's names isn't the same as being friends with them. It really hurts to be without a friend when you've had someone like Tim all your life.

I've known Tim for as long as I can remember, and we've been friends all that time. As to our shoving matches, neither of us ever thought they were for real. Leaving Tim had been the hardest part of the whole move. I figured I could get used to a new school and learn to find my way around a different town, but you just don't replace friends like so many alkaline batteries.

What with getting ready for Christmas and having the stationery and cards and ads printed to start her new studio, Mom didn't have much time to stand around and chatter. Since DeeDee and I are both used to a mother with a business of her own, we are pretty good at amusing ourselves.

And Grissi really helped amuse everybody. Even when he was somewhere else in the house, I was conscious of him. Everybody talked to him, not just Dad. I would hear DeeDee off in her room chattering away and could almost see Grissi, his head cocked, listening. It was a good thing that cats don't talk or he could have told everyone what DeeDee was giving them for Christmas.

DeeDee adores presents. She honestly likes to give them as much as she likes receiving them. She started Christmas shopping before we finished the last soup Mom had made from the bones of the Thanksgiving turkey.

By then DeeDee was allowed to go down to the store by herself, and she thought of some reason to go almost every day. She knew everyone in the whole neighborhood and chattered on about them all the time at home.

Since sixth graders get about twice as much homework as second graders do, I spent a lot of time up at my desk. I was supposed to be studying, but I looked out the window a lot and drew pictures. The minute DeeDee left the house, Grissi would come to keep me company. I drew a lot of pictures of that cat when I should have been sticking to my homework.

Night comes early in December. Would you believe no stars? Well, that's not fair. Once in a while, on a very clear night, I saw one or two lonely little sparks out there, but they sure didn't cluster in the sky the way they did back in Peoria. Maybe the stars didn't feel any more at home in Brooklyn than I did.

Instead, from my window, I saw some spotlights from people's backyards bathing the gardens below with an eerie green glow. Street lamps marched along the part of the block I could see at one end of the alley, but the sky, instead of being prickled with stars, was lit with a dull red glow.

Although back home that glow would have gone with sunset, Tim and I would have wheeled together through the neighborhood for as long as it lasted, watching the lights go on in houses and seeing the neighbors' cats let out for the night. Just thinking about Tim hurt enough that I'd grab something to work on really hard.

During those weeks, I discovered how much more difficult it is to draw live things than dead ones. Sometimes Grissi would curl up on my bed and purr contentedly, his eyes only half closed for fear he might miss something. Other days he would sit on my windowsill and watch the pigeons or stare down into the garden. When something set that dark dog, Butch, to barking, Grissi would stand up and narrow his eyes. A ridge of hair would rise along his spine like the horns on the back of a lizard or dinosaur, and his eyes would narrow to slits.

Before long I had a huge stack of sketches of Grissi. I let Mom choose which ones were good enough to do in watercolor.

The people with the rose garden were named Larson. They looked alike, both small, round people who wore knitted hats and mittens when they were outside. One afternoon I watched them, wearing matching mufflers, string lights in that little cone-shaped tree in their garden. After that, every afternoon promptly at five, Mrs. Larson came out all wrapped up and turned the tree lights on.

The Joons next to us hung a marvelous wreath on their door. The whole thing was made of pinecones tipped in white. When the wind was coming from the right direction, I could hear the muted clanging of bells from the direction of the church. People wearing Santa suits stood there on the corner collecting money for charity, no matter how cold it got. All those people looked alike to me in those red suits, but DeeDee knew them all by name and how many children each one had.

Christmas picks up speed as it gets nearer. The post office and UPS trucks began to deliver packages from family and friends back in Illinois. Grissi always waited eagerly in the hall while Mom signed for deliveries. It's silly to think you can read a cat's mind, but I'm sure he knew that the wrapping paper would be his to roll in and chase and pounce on after the gifts were taken out. I laughed myself into hiccups a couple of times when he got so hopelessly tangled in the paper and rope that we had to help him get free again.

But all that time I just wanted to go back home.

Dad took Mom to a bunch of parties in lower Manhattan across the East River that were given by his firm. DeeDee's friends came by and they made Christmas cards together. I sat in my room a lot, drawing more pictures of Grissi and listening to that dark dog bark.

If this sounds dull to you, it was worse than dull. Nobody's ever going to make up a song about a Black Christmas, but that was what that one was for me.

In fact, I can remember only three good things about that Christmas. Putting the tree up was more fun than I can ever remember. Grissi was enchanted by the ornaments. He would stare at one a while, then whap it with his paw and send it flying. His chase around the room and through the wrapped packages under the tree while knocking those balls around was hilarious. Finally Mom gave up and bought special unbreakable ornaments to hang as far up as Grissi could reach.

DeeDee bought a little red-and-green stocking for Grissi and put a catnip mouse in it. Grissi went wild, dragging that stocking around in his teeth, rolling on it or crawling toward it on his belly until he was close enough to pounce.

DeeDee didn't put on that good a show, but she was really crazy about the framed watercolor of Grissi that I gave her. And Mom, who knows about art, offered to hang it in the big front room on the parlor floor. When your art work graduates from being fastened to the refrigerator door with a magnet to being hung in the living room, you've come up in the world at our house.

The other exciting thing was a set of opaque water colors that Mom got me. This was a whole new medium for me. These watercolors were really strange because there weren't any colors at all, just black and white and three shades of gray. You weren't supposed to let the shades run together like regular watercolors. Instead you studied the different tones of the shadows. By painting them the exact proper shades, whatever you were drawing leaped into life.

The snow that should have come a week earlier began to fall during the night of New Year's Eve. Fine flakes were still spinning past my window when I woke up that first morning of the new year. The snowplows started coming through about ten, clanking and rattling along the streets and alleys. By noon, our garden looked like mashed potatoes, with great lustrous lumps of white that totally concealed the path and the bushes. The concrete bench looked overstuffed, and the birch trees were tufted with white.

I bundled up to go try to draw the drifts in the garden with those new paints of mine. I passed by the kitchen on my way down to the basement floor where the back door was. Grissi was crouching over his bowl in the kitchen as I went by, sorting out some dried food that DeeDee had given him for Christmas. The nuggets came in various shapes and flavors and he was particular about which ones he ate. He crunched away happily through his favorites but set the ones he didn't like out on the floor around his dish. He looked so busy that I didn't even think he saw me.

That dog, Butch, began to bark wildly the way he did every time anyone went out our back door. I heard someone yell at him, but that wasn't too unusual either. I had brushed the snow off a patio chair and was drawing the bench when I heard our back door open. I didn't even look around. I just figured it was DeeDee following me out. I was concentrating on how to show the bench by painting only the shadows, leaving the paper white behind it to be the snow.

"He likes it," DeeDee said in this happy voice.

I turned around to see Grissi picking his way delicately along the walk, lifting his feet up in an exaggerated fashion and looking this way and that as if he had been put down on a strange new planet.

DeeDee, who hadn't stopped for her jacket, came and stood by me anyway, wrapping her arms around herself for extra warmth.

I'll never forget that moment. It stays in my mind, frozen like a TV still, the two of us watching Grissi in such a relaxed way, just enjoying him.

The cat made his way along the snowy path, looked up at the fence, and picked his way toward it. He had leaped for the crossbar before I figured out what was in his mind.

DeeDee called out in a sudden panicky voice, "No, Grissi," she cried. "Come back, come back."

I scattered paints in all directions, trying to get over to him.

5

Captain Jinks

I don't think Grissi meant to run away. I think he just wanted to be on top of the fence where he could see better. But I was conscious that beyond that fence lay the alley, where there could be danger. Loving something makes you very conscious of danger.

There's no point in denying that being yelled at startled the gray cat. Just as he hit that fence, he glanced back at us, lost his balance, and plunged from view on the alley side.

DeeDee was under my feet when I hit the gate. Everything works against you when you are really in a hurry. First the latch wouldn't lift. When I finally scraped it upward, the gate wouldn't budge. I had to throw my whole weight against it to shove away the snow that had been piled up against it when the snowplow went through the alley.

I was so busy trying to get out to Grissi that it didn't

register on me that the eternal barking of that Butch had changed its tone. Just as DeeDee and I tumbled out into the drift by the gate, that dog shot past us, chasing Grissi, who ran for his life down the alley.

Butch was gaining on him with DeeDee and me right behind when Grissi swerved, jumped for a garbage can, and then onto the roof of the potting shed behind the Larson house.

DeeDee was screaming and I was shouting at the dog to heel. We should have saved our breath. Butch didn't pay any attention until Grissi got away. Then he skidded to a stop and stared from us to the spot on the roof of the shed where he had last seen the cat.

"Catch him, catch Butch," we could hear a man yelling as he ran hatless down the alley after us. "Grab his collar," he shouted. "Catch him while you can."

I reached for Butch's collar, only to have him back off, growling and baring his teeth at me. Then his owner was there, explaining that the dog had jumped the fence from a snowbank.

I didn't care how Butch had got out or whether the man had him back or anything. I only cared about Grissi.

"Quick," I told DeeDee. "Run through our house and knock at the Larson's front door. I'll try to get in by the alley gate."

She was sobbing as she ran off into the house.

"I'm really sorry," the man said, holding his dog, which kept lunging toward me, jerking his arm as he gripped the animal's collar.

I wanted to scream at him, to tell him to get lost and take his big, noisy, stupid dog with him. But that wouldn't have done any good. I just turned away and ran to the Larsons' back gate.

Naturally the gate was locked. I scrambled up on a snowy garbage can and hung onto the roof of the shed to try to see into the garden.

Grissi had hit the yard not far from the shed. His streak of a trail went between those tied white bushes, which had turned to ghostly mounds under the snow. I could see where he had skidded, changing direction. Then the tracks stopped, all at once, as if Grissi had been swallowed up by something.

My heart fell.

Grissi hadn't stopped there and been swallowed up. I could just see him gathering himself up for another of those great leaps. That one would have taken him to the top of the fence and over it into the next yard, still running.

Deedee was wasting her time bothering the Larsons. Grissi was off somewhere and there was no telling what direction he had taken.

I have always been envious of the way that DeeDee can make friends. That day I was grateful for it. Mr. and Mrs. Larson looked genuinely heartbroken when they came out with DeeDee to search the yard.

Seen close up, the Larsons didn't look nearly that much alike. Mrs. Larson was a little pudding of a lady with a

54

puffy, white-hooded jacket thrown over a silk dress. She was so upset that her face was all squinched in around her glasses. She kept patting DeeDee and saying, "My dear, my poor dear."

Everybody got into the search that afternoon. Mom and Dad went from door to door along the block in the direction Grissi had taken. DeeDee and I covered the houses across the street and then went along the block where the shops are. A lot of the stores were closed for New Year's Day, but every merchant whose store was open seemed to know DeeDee and all about Grissi and promised to watch for him.

Then it began to get dark and I knew we had better go back before Mom and Dad came looking for us.

"But we can't go home," DeeDee wailed. "I won't go home without Grissi. He's out here and he's cold. There are cars . . . "

She left that sentence unfinished and burst into tears.

Of course she did go home. We all did. Dad tried to cheer everyone up by talking about running ads and trying again in the morning. Mom cooked dinner with her back to us and it sounded as if she had caught a cold. I kept reminding Dee Dee that Grissi had been a street cat once and would know how to take care of himself. I hoped I was right.

We were just sitting down for dinner when the doorbell rang. DeeDee and I both shot to our feet and scrambled for the hall, with Mom calling after us to be careful. I know that DeeDee was thinking the same thing I was, that somebody had found Grissi and would be standing there at the door, bringing him home.

The man at our door probably looked shorter than he really was because we were at the top of the big stoop and he had stepped back down onto the sidewalk. But even making allowance for that, he looked broader than he looked tall. And he looked terribly old. I don't mean *very* old, I mean *terribly* old. His face was a strange, putty color that made him look sick as well as worn out. His wide gray pants ballooned around his ankles without the sign of a crease. The pockets on his loose jacket were so crammed with something heavy that they dragged down on the sides, below the hem. That jacket looked as if it had begun the same color as the pants, but now it was dark and stained around the cuffs.

He was hatless. Long strands of white hair had been pulled over his bald head from the left side to the right. The scalp under those strands of hair was the same sickly color as his face. The hair that had gone from his head seemed to have gathered in a great bush on his chin.

DeeDee shoved around me and cried out to him in recognition. "Captain," she said. "This awful thing! Grissi ran away."

He nodded. "They told me. I'm so sorry. But he didn't really run away, you know. He was chased away. That's different." His eyes were gentle.

"But he's gone," she wailed. "We've looked everywhere."

He nodded again, in a reassuring way, still without smiling. "I wanted you to know I'll search for him, too." He paused. "But you might watch the iron yard. That's where they go, you know, when they have no place else."

"The iron yard?" I asked. "Where is it?"

He looked at me with amazement. "Everyone knows where the iron yard is," he said. "The iron yard," he repeated, nodding.

"Thank you, Captain," DeeDee said. "Thank you so much."

By the time the man was a few doors away, his pockets swaying back and forth as he walked, Mom and Dad were there behind us.

"Who was that? What did he want?" Dad asked, staring after him.

"That's Captain Jinks," DeeDee said in a matter-of-fact way.

"Is this some kind of a joke?" Dad asked.

She shook her head. "Everybody knows Captain. He gave me Grissi, you know. He asked us if we had looked in the iron yard."

"Where's that?" Dad asked.

"It's supposed to be over behind the church on that side street," DeeDee said. "Can we go right now?"

Mom lifted her eyebrows the way she does. "Who's hungry?" she said. "Boots, though. Everybody has to wear boots, no exceptions."

6

The Iron Yard

That was a black-and-white night with hardly any grays. The sky was dark and starless. The light from the street lamps glistened on mounds of fresh snow. We walked along with our heads wreathed in our own white breath.

I can never predict how DeeDee is going to act. She is usually all over everybody, banging against us, putting her face up for kisses, sliding in under Dad's or Mom's arm. That night she walked apart from all of us, as if the loss of Grissi were something she couldn't even share.

Shovels scraped everywhere, including along the walk by the church, where Dad stopped in indecision. The man pushing the shovel around was almost buried in a giant scarf that hung down his back almost to his waist. He stopped his shovel to look up as we approached. Then, at the sight of DeeDee, he smiled and rested his weight on his shovel. "Good evening, Miss Double Dee," he said very formally. "It's a chill night for a stroll."

"Hi, Mr. Farley," she said, tightening her mouth against tears. "We're looking for my cat."

"Not the new cat with the yellow eyes?" he said, glancing at Dad with a distressed expression.

"The same," Dad said, extending his hand. "I see you know my daughter. I'm Chris Gregory, Mr. Farley. A man named Jinks suggested we look in the iron yard. Could you tell us where that is?"

"Pleasure, I'm sure," Mr. Farley said, shaking Dad's hand. "You're smart to try the iron yard. And the Captain should know."

I saw Mom and Dad trade glances as Mr. Farley set his shovel against the stone wall and started toward the corner. "Down there," he said, pointing along the quiet street that ran behind the church. "Past the church and those buildings, there's an empty lot. It was an iron yard some time ago." His smile was quick and radiant. "Beautiful things came out of that place. Some of the handsomest homes in this city boast work that came from that very iron yard." Then, remembering, he touched Dee-Dee's shoulder. "Good hunting, Miss Double Dee."

She nodded and shot off so fast that Dad barely got his thanks out before we had to race after her.

The buildings Mr. Farley mentioned seemed to be the backs of things. They had only high, dark windows with grills over them and solid, single doors opening along the street.

The houses across the street could not have been more different. They were only two stories tall, and all across their fronts were wide, big windows almost like doors that glowed with light through drawn curtains. The curved iron work of the front fences were frosted with snow. A dog began to bark as we passed, a dog with a deep, rich bark like a German shepherd. I saw a curtain twitch as if someone were peering out to see what had startled the dog.

When we caught up with DeeDee, she was standing on the sidewalk staring into a big, untidy lot. Buildings rose around it on three sides, leaving a dark, cluttered square, poorly lit by two hooded lights with cages over the bulbs. Metal fire escapes staggered up the sides of all the buildings, and here and there around the lot were dark mysterious mounds of snow that gave no clue to what was underneath. I realized that one pile of snow was covering one of those dumpsters full of refuse that are brought and carried away on trucks. The cab of a truck with two flat tires was parked along one wall. The pile across from it looked like abandoned shelves.

Against the other wall were piled what little there was left to show that this had been an iron works. Broken pieces of grill work, some iron bars to cover basement windows, and an archway from a Victorian garden were jumbled all together under the snow. Only a garden bench, lacking one leg and frosted with snow, relieved the bleakness of this dark mass against the white-painted bricks of the building.

Although nobody had shoveled there, footprints in the snow revealed that someone had come, walked to the middle of the open area, and then left, almost retracing his steps.

DeeDee ran to where the footsteps stopped and knelt down. I followed her and saw her looking at the pattern of trampled snow around the footsteps.

I can't explain how spooky it was there in the dark and cold. Even by the weak light of those two high lamps, we could see marks on the snow in a design like a spider web, with DeeDee and me in the center. But the threads spinning out from where we stood were not lines at all but the traces of tiny animal feet.

Yet, as DeeDee and I stood there staring around us, there wasn't a single sign or sound of life anywhere.

"Grissi," she called softly, staring at the snow-buried things around the yard. "Grissi?"

The wanting in her voice hurt. As I watched, she tugged off one mitten with her teeth and fished a plastic bag out of the front of her jacket. Cat food.

"Grissi," she coaxed. "Come. Eat."

I think Mom and Dad must have been holding their breaths like I was. It was that quiet. Then we heard it, a small answering *mew* from somewhere up high. It wasn't Grissi's *mur-r-rr*, but a higher, querulous sound like that of a Siamese. I looked up and grabbed DeeDee's arm, afraid to speak for fear I would frighten the animal away.

Coming down a fire escape, one careful step at a time, and mewing with every move, was a cat as thin as a book without pictures. Reaching the ground, the little Sia-

mese princess paused, studied DeeDee a minute, then came swiftly toward her, tail waving straight up.

DeeDee glanced at me, then offered the cat some of the food on her open palm. The cat took it delicately, as Grissi always did, turning her head to catch the nugget between side teeth. Then she hunched on the snow to eat.

"I guess we can go," DeeDee said. "Grissi isn't here."

"Wait," I whispered. "Wait."

Suddenly I understood the weblike pattern of tiny feet. All around us, some sitting and studying us, some getting up their nerve to join the little princess, were cats.

I have never seen that many cats, nor that many colors of cats. A beautiful short-legged cat with a wide, heavy belly and off-white fur came next. In spite of her weight, she flowed across the lot like running water. She stopped at DeeDee's side and looked up silently with startlingly blue eyes.

I didn't even count them that night, but one calico cat with golden eyes rubbed against my legs and purred so powerfully that I could feel her vibrate. One of them was so jowly and fat that he rolled when he walked like a sailor in a cartoon. Although DeeDee stood in a moving sea of cats, more eyes still glinted at us from the darkness. "That's all the food I brought," DeeDee wailed, when she had emptied the plastic bag.

Dad and Mom had stayed huddled together on the sidewalk. "We know what the Captain meant now, honey,"

Dad called to DeeDee. "This must be the place where stray cats come to be fed. You and Peter can watch here. Maybe Grissi will come."

DeeDee left reluctantly, looking back. The talkative little princess who had been the first to eat followed us. She walked along with her tail high and her head tilted regally. At the corner, after a final mew, she turned to go back with the others. Mr. Farley had finished shoveling the church walk and gone back inside his little caretaker's apartment. The four of us walked home in silence.

Mom had been right about nobody's being hungry.

That night we did the same things as usual but more quietly. DeeDee set out place mats, and I got down dishes and filled milk glasses while Mom tossed the salad and made gravy to go with the pot roast. It was as if each of us had withdrawn to some private place apart.

"There's something almost magical about that place," Dad said when we were all sitting quietly over our plates. "Maybe we just went there the right night."

"Magic," DeeDee repeated. "I always used to have my three wishes picked out in case somebody with magic offers them. Now they are all the same wish."

Her words jarred me. I thought I was the only kid who listened to those fairy tales about people ruining their three wishes and promptly got my own ready, just in case.

"All of us have the same three wishes tonight,"

Mom told her. "But we still have to get some sleep."

Upstairs the pigeons along my window ledge had settled down and Butch, for a wonder, had quit barking. I didn't have any excuse to lie awake as long as I did.

I thought I did a pretty good job of keeping my mind on what I was doing that next day in school. When Mr. Lazarus closed his book and called my name near the end of the last period, I jumped in my seat.

"Yes, sir," I said, feeling guilty for no reason.

"You clearly haven't been yourself today, Peter," he said. "Now, it has come to my attention that your family had some misfortune yesterday. Want to tell your classmates about it? They might be able to help."

I was almost too startled to answer. How did he know? Who had told him?

To this day I can't remember what I said as I stumbled to my feet. I know I told them what a great cat Grissi was and how long and hard we had looked for him. Whatever I said made the room very quiet for a long minute.

That wasn't the first time those kids had stared at me. It was only the first time they had stared at me while I was looking. Funny thing, only Hal and his buddies kept their eyes on their desks, fiddling with things.

I watched the other kids and could almost feel them think. Then the red-haired girl whose name is Stacy or Tracy or Lacy Casey, I never quite caught it, held up her hand.

66

"That's awful," she said. "I couldn't stand it if I lost my dog. I wish I had seen your cat so I'd know what I was looking for."

The whole class broke out with stories of their own animals, of how they had been lost and then found, of places to look, of newspapers that would carry free "lost" ads. Mr. Lazarus listened, letting this just go on for a long time. Then Tim, who sits two seats over and one up from me, looped his arm over the back of his chair and turned to speak directly to me.

"You must have some snapshots," he said. "Cats don't look all that much alike. If we could see his picture, we'd be able to recognize him."

"Good thinking, Tim," Mr. Lazarus said. "Could you bring photos of your cat, Peter?"

I knew it was a good idea. Unfortunately, I also knew that the box with the camera equipment in it was one we had decided could wait a while to get unpacked. I even knew where it was, because I had moved it to get some games out during the holidays. I hesitated, then said, "I wish we had pictures of Grissi, but we don't."

"Well!" Mr. Lazarus paused. "That's too bad, because it was a good idea." Then he pushed back his cuff and checked his watch against the clock on the wall. "Now let's see how many of you can hold your breath until the final bell rings."

Every time he plays that game with the class, somebody explodes before the bell sounds. None of my teachers back in Illinois ever did that. It's great because that way everybody leaves in a good mood.

When I got outside I realized the wind had shifted into the south and the snow was melting fast. I had figured that DeeDee would want to run all the way home. Instead, she looked all the way home. We even had to go down that alley where she had first found Grissi and call and call for him a long time.

Mrs. Joon was passing our house on her way home from her office. When she saw us coming, she slowed down to let us catch up with her.

"DeeDee," she called in that wonderful accent. "Have you found your beautiful Grissi?"

"Not yet," DeeDee told her. Then she paused. "But, oh, Mrs. Joon, you should see the lost cat we found last night. She looks just like you. I mean, she makes me think of you."

Mrs. Joon's astonishment turned into laughter.

"She is Eastern and carries a briefcase, this cat?" she asked.

DeeDee shook her head. "She's very dainty and small. She walks like a princess and has a high, clear voice."

Mrs. Joon giggled. "I must practice my princess walk. Some day you will show me this princess cat."

"You'll love her," DeeDee predicted.

7
Colin Cramar

DeeDee rushed ahead of me to the kitchen. I knew what she was hoping, but there was no gray cat curled on the windowsill shelf.

Mom insisted that we eat something before going to the iron yard. Then she had a list of things she wanted us to bring back from the drugstore. By this time, DeeDee was dancing with impatience.

It looked to me as if Mom were stalling, trying to keep DeeDee from going. I thought I knew what Mom was thinking, because I had worried about the same thing all the way home from school.

DeeDee had lived on the hope of finding Grissi in the iron yard for a whole night and a day now. Her face looked thinner and her eyes bigger already. Every hour we didn't find Grissi, I could feel my own confidence melting away. I didn't know how DeeDee was going to deal with having her hopes dashed again.

"Mama!" DeeDee finally squealed. "It'll be dark again before we even get there."

Mom sighed. "All right. The things from the drugstore aren't that important. But don't wait until dark to come home."

Mr. Farley saw us passing the church and stepped out. "Any luck last night?" he asked DeeDee.

She shook her head. "We're going to look again." Then she added, "There are some wonderful cats there, but none of them is mine."

"Wonderful cats?" he asked, smiling at her the way people always do at DeeDee. "How can you tell a wonderful cat?"

"Personality," she told him. "Just like people."

He laughed. "Maybe you should find us a church cat to go with our church mouse."

He winked at me as he said it, sure that I had heard the phrase "as poor as a church mouse."

That small street had been empty the night before. Now, as we passed the church, I saw a boy walking ahead of us in the direction of the iron yard. I realized right away that it was Colin Cramar. I didn't think anything about his being there. He had to live around the neighborhood somewhere. I kept seeing him all the time, even though he never seemed to see me.

I expected Colin to go on down the street to wherever he lived. Instead, before he even reached the iron yard, cats came running out to him as if he had given some invisible signal. They came from every direction to mill about him, mewing and rubbing against his legs.

I put my hand on DeeDee's arm to stop her. I guess I just wanted to see what he was going to do.

I had never seen Colin Cramar smile and I certainly had not heard him talk the way he did to those cats. This was nothing like that flat, all-on-one-level kind of voice he always used at school.

I couldn't hear his words, but his tone sounded as if he were talking to a bunch of old friends who had a lot to say back. You could hear that slender cat with the Siamese voice over all the rest of them, even though the others were singing up a chorus around Colin's legs.

As we watched, Colin slid the knapsack off his shoulders and laid it on the ground. He pulled out a big bag of cat food and poured it in a huge circle with himself in the middle. Not until he was joining the ends of that circle did he glance our way and see us watching him. He stopped and stood very still, as if he had been caught doing something bad. His smile left swiftly, leaving an angry, surly look on his face.

I just stayed where I was, but DeeDee started toward him, walking carefully so as not to scare the cats.

"I guess you're looking for your lost one," he said to her.

She nodded, glancing all around that crouching ring of cats. "He's not here," she told him. "He wasn't here last night, either. My name's DeeDee Gregory."

He nodded in a jerky, embarrassed way, glancing over at me as if he were angry at me. "I'm Colin Cramar."

"Do you always feed these cats?" she asked, kneeling down to watch them. They stayed in their places at that circular ring of food, eating warily, keeping an eye on her.

"Not always," he said. When she looked up at him, he nodded. "A lot of the time." Then after a minute, "Every school day."

She watched him thoughtfully. "Somebody had been here yesterday feeding them."

He nodded. "Captain Jinks does it on the weekends."

She nodded soberly. Then, looking down at the cats again, she asked, "They all know you, don't they?"

He hadn't looked at me again. Like Hal, he must have decided I was invisible. "Some of them have been here a long time," he told her.

Then he pointed at a big cat I hadn't noticed the night before. "That's Bumble," he told her. "I understand he comes from a long line of losers. He's awkward and funny and doesn't do anything right, but he's a neat guy, anyway."

DeeDee was staring at the cat curiously. "What does he do wrong?"

For a minute I thought Colin was going to smile again. "Everything," he told her. "The other cats creep on their stomachs when they hunt. Not old Bumble. He'll run at a bird mewing like crazy. I don't think he's ever caught even a pigeon in his whole life. And fences," Colin went

72

on, his voice rising a little. "Bumble has fallen off every fence in this neighborhood. He never seems to get hurt. He just sits and blinks, shakes his head, and climbs up to fall again. His dad was called Bonkers and was supposed to be the same exact way."

DeeDee giggled softly. "I like him," she decided out loud. "Do they all have names?"

He nodded. "That tall, silvery one with the golden spot on her chest is Moonshine."

You would have thought Colin didn't know I was there, as he went on talking to DeeDee. Sometimes a cat looked up when he spoke. Mostly they just went on eating, as if cleaning away that circle of food was a contest with a big prize at the end.

There was Rowdy, a tiger-striped gray cat who ate with his tail straight in the air like a flag on a pole. The only one who had run away when DeeDee came up was a cat named Sweet Pete. He had come back right away, but he watched her with scared green eyes all the time he ate.

The fat one was Guinness. "Because he is stout." Unk was the old one with patches of fur gone and one ear bent like a wonton.

"And the talky one?" DeeDee asked.

"That's Miss O," Colin said, without explaining the name. "And this one is Cream." He pointed to the pale, broad one that moved so flowingly. "She's about to have kittens."

"Out here?" Deedee asked, looking distressed. "Without any home?"

74

Colin shrugged and picked up his backpack. "Home is what you've got," he told her. "This is all they have, until the right owner comes along. *If*," he corrected himself.

"Like I did for Grissi," she said.

He nodded and almost smiled.

"How did the Captain know I was right?" she asked.

This time he did smile. "You know," he said. "You just know."

She looked down at that contented circle of cats. Moonshine had finished and was licking the golden spot on her chest as if she had spilled something on her bib and had to clean it. Cream was still munching hungrily, as if she had to eat for her coming kittens as well as herself.

"It would be nice to find people for all of these," she said.

"Nice." He nodded. "Very nice."

Ever since that second day of school, when Hal and his henchmen started teasing me, I had blamed Colin Cramer for my trouble. He was the only person who had ever seen me doing the baby-sitter operation. He had to have told everybody right off, to start that teasing before anyone else even knew I had a little sister.

That didn't seem important any more. Now there were other things I wanted to ask him, about Captain Jinks, and how Colin himself had gotten into feeding the iron-yard cats. Something about his manner made me even shyer than usual. He slid his backpack onto his shoulders and started on down the street. Then he looked back at DeeDee. "I hope you find your cat," he said.

He was halfway to the corner before I got my courage up. "Wait here for me, DeeDee," I told her and ran to catch up with him.

He stopped as if he didn't want me walking along with him. When he looked at me like that, I didn't know what to say. He didn't wait for me to make up my mind.

"You think I started all that teasing business with Sanders and his goons, don't you?" he challenged.

I felt color come to my face for no reason. Maybe I don't like having my mind read. "Somebody had to tell them that I was baby-sitting that bunch of little girls. Nobody saw me with them but you."

"Are you ashamed of your sister or something?" he asked.

"It's not that," I began. Then I realized what I was doing. He had gotten me into all that trouble with the teasing and the fight, and here I was, being defensive about blaming him. How had he turned it around to make it my fault?

"Listen," I said. "Don't come at me like that. It was rotten of you to run back there and tell everybody."

He shook his head. "I just told them why you hadn't come when I asked you to join us. They had decided you were stuck-up, eating all by yourself, and then going off like that without explaining why to anyone." He shook his head again, in an irritated way. "I don't get you at all. You must be putting on some kind of an act."

76

I honestly think there must be something in the air in Brooklyn that brings out the fighter in me. I didn't even understand why he was saying that but it made me want to hit him. Put on an act?

"I guess you would really like it if I told everybody you went around babying a bunch of stray cats."

He turned and stared at me. Then he laughed, a short laugh that didn't have any humor in it. "I don't do things I'm ashamed of," he told me. "I'm not out to prove anything."

That time he really left. Staring after him, I felt more ashamed than angry. I wanted to call him back and explain myself to him, make him see me differently. But my own head was fuzzy about what I could possibly say. I wasn't ashamed of DeeDee, or of being from Peoria, but those things somehow didn't fit in with the way I wanted to be understood. I shrugged. It was just as well I didn't catch up with him. I didn't know what I meant clearly enough to be able to put it into words for myself, much less him.

Before DeeDee and I left the iron yard, all the cats except Sweet Pete had let DeeDee pet them. It was starting to get dark and I made her come home with me, even though she wasn't ready. I finally set off walking ahead, with her dragging behind the way she almost always does.

When we were a good part of the way home, I looked around and realized that Miss O was still following us.

I was about to yell at DeeDee when it occurred to me

that maybe she had already given up on finding Grissi. If this was the case, maybe she was bringing Miss O home in hopes that Mom would let her stay.

I could still remember that painful rhythm of her sobbing the night before. Maybe it would even be healthy for her to get another cat right away.

Instead, when we reached our door, she called to me, "I'll be there in a minute, Peter."

As I turned to argue, she knelt, picked up Miss O, and marched on up the street. Before I could get a word out, DeeDee had rung the bell at the Joon house.

The light from the big double parlor-floor door spread a fan shape of brilliance onto the stoop. Mrs. Joon was wearing an amazing shade of red, somewhere between pure carmine and orange.

When she bent to look at the cat in DeeDee's arms, she seemed as skinny as a piece of red paper herself. After only a minute, DeeDee set Miss O down. Since I couldn't hear a thing, it was like watching a scene from a silent movie. I saw the cat and Mrs. Joon looking at each other, then Miss O leaning her slenderness against the skirt of that red dress, head tilted up, talking. The happy ending came when Mrs. Joon knelt and picked up Miss O in her arms.

As DeeDee skipped back toward our house, Mrs. Joon was still standing there in that fan of light, smiling, with Miss O against her shoulder.

"Well, that was quite a performance," I told DeeDee. "What if Mrs. Joon hadn't wanted a cat?"

"Oh, she didn't," DeeDee said. "Or she didn't think she did until she saw the right one."

She grinned up at me and ducked under my arm as I held the door to the basement where Mom was getting her studio all set up.

DeeDee clattered up the stairs after Mom and I could hear her voice in the kitchen.

"We didn't find Grissi yet," she was saying. "But I have the most wonderful new friend. His name is Colin."

I wished she hadn't mentioned Colin's name. It brought back all those confused feelings I'd had when he walked away. Even with the light still on and the sound of Mom and DeeDee talking upstairs, I felt bleak and lonely there in the basement hall by myself.

8

The Message

DeeDee has never been an early riser. She's always been that kind of kid who has to be hauled out of bed and led like a zombie through the first couple of hours of every day.

After Grissi disappeared, all that changed. When I'd get downstairs for breakfast, she'd be already there, dressed for school. She looked even smaller and skinnier than usual the next morning. She didn't even glance up when I came in. Instead, she sat staring at nothing over a half-filled cereal bowl.

Mom caught my eye and shook her head, warning me not to say anything. Not until DeeDee dragged off upstairs for her school satchel did Mom explain.

"That poor little kid," Mom said. "She really is taking the loss of her cat hard. She says she wakes up hearing him crying outside. Then she goes to the window, but no cat is out there."

"Do you think she dreams it?" I asked.

Mom sighed. "Maybe so. She doesn't seem to think about much else. Yet what can we do?"

When I told Mom about the kids at school wanting to see snapshots of Grissi so they could help look, she turned to me with sudden brightness. "What a good idea. And that's awfully nice of them. It's certainly worth a try."

"Only we haven't any snapshots," I reminded her.

"But you have those sketches you made," she protested. "They are lots better than any photo could be."

"I thought of them," I admitted. "But they all have my initials at the bottom in ink. You know the way I mark them."

"So?" she asked.

"So I'm not going in there with an armful of pictures with my name on them."

She looked at me a long minute, then shook her head. "I guess you don't have to understand a kid to love him," she said. Then, "You can't possibly be ashamed of that work. Why not take it to school?"

"And start a whole new storm of teasing?" I asked her.

"You'd let a little teasing keep you from trying to help DeeDee out of this hole she's in?" she asked, with disbelief in her voice. "And anyway, you do draw, you are an artist—why try to hide it?"

"You don't understand," I protested.

"That's what I already told you," she said, a little snappishly this time. "I really don't understand you at all."

Mom has a way of making you feel that anything she

doesn't understand, she doesn't like. By the time DeeDee and I were ready to start off for school, I had given in and packed a bunch of my drawings to take along. When DeeDee eyed the package curiously, I told her what Tim had suggested.

"Oh," she cried. "Could I have some to take to my class, too?"

"If you promise just to show the pictures and not tell where you got them," I said.

"Why?" she asked.

"Because that's the way I want it," I told her, taking the top two sketches off and handing them to her. "Nobody wants to be a show-and-tell exhibit for the whole second grade."

"Oh, I'd like that," she said.

I groaned, realizing that she probably would.

Her two little friends caught up with us a block from school, and the three girls went on ahead. I saw DeeDee stop on the front steps and talk to Colin a minute, but that didn't register until I took the drawings up to Mr. Lazarus' desk.

The kids whose seats were nearby stood up in their places to stare as Mr. Lazarus spread the pages out. "Nice," he said. "These are really nice, Peter. Who's the artist in your family?"

He had asked the question exactly as I hoped he would. "My mother is an artist," I told him. "She's an interior decorator."

83

"And she did these?" he asked, looking up from them to meet my eyes.

He was not the only person watching and listening. Colin was sitting two seats back, taking all this in. He had his head cocked a little, as if the weight of his thoughts had unbalanced his head. He was waiting—I could see him waiting for me to lie about those pictures. After all, DeeDee had stopped him out in front. I could almost hear her telling him that she had brought pictures of Grissi that I had drawn. "I don't do things I am ashamed of," he had said. I felt a rush of heat to my face and knew that I was blushing.

"No," I told him. "I did these."

Mr. Lazarus' expression changed as he looked at me steadily for a moment. Then he nodded. "They are re-markable, Peter," he said. "They are really remarkable. It must be hard to draw like this from life."

"It is," I told him. A whole bunch of the kids had gathered around the desk and were really admiring the pictures. Instead of being proud, I was embarrassed. "But I'm not an artist. I can only draw things that I see."

Snicker. Naturally it was Hal Sanders, back in his seat, pulling the sides of his mouth down and jiggling his shoulders as he repeated, "Can only draw things that I see."

"I'm going to have to think about that remark," Mr. Lazarus said. Then, looking sternly at Hal, he added, "Most of us would settle for being able to draw what we can see half this well."

"Can you just put them up and not say who did them?" I asked quietly.

He looked at me again steadily. "If that's the way you want it."

We both knew it was too late for that. When the kids stared at the pictures and then at me, I slumped down in my seat as far as I could go. I was absolutely positive I was in for a fresh epidemic of teasing because of those drawings.

That was the strangest day. Kids who had never said a word before came up and talked to me. It turned out that Stacy's father was a commercial artist. She promised to bring me a children's book he had illustrated. Standing close to her like that, I realized that her hair wasn't really red but coppery colored, like the bottom of a freshly polished pan.

Stephen told me he had a computer at home that he could draw designs on in color.

"It's easy," he said. "And really fun. Some day after you see your little sister home, come over and try it."

I watched his face when he said that. He didn't seem to think there was anything so bad about seeing a kid home, either. I told him I'd like to but wouldn't be doing much of anything until we found Grissi.

"Have you talked to Captain Jinks?" he asked. "My dad says he knows every cat in downtown Brooklyn." When he grinned, his face changed shape from a triangle to a round wad with teeth. "In fact, Dad says that if Captain had his way, he would find homes for every stray cat in the world."

I told how Captain had given Grissi to DeeDee in the first place.

"That's a real compliment." He nodded. "Captain is very particular who he gives cats to."

I meant to tell DeeDee what Stephen had said right away, but she and her little people came flying out of the building after school faster than they had ever made it before. DeeDee looked like her old self, eyes sparkling, her cheeks all pink with excitement.

"Somebody's found Grissi!" she said. "Look at this. I got a note."

"Who sent it?" I asked, unfolding the piece of grubby notebook paper she handed me.

"I don't know," she said. "It was just on my desk after lunch. Look, there's an address and everything. Can we go right now?"

I stared at the note. It was in a kid's handwriting, the letters little and cramped and bent to the left. All it said was, "You can find your cat at—" and then the address.

"I haven't any idea where this place is," I told her. "And anyway, we have to check in with Mom first."

The tears began then, real tears. "Maybe he'll leave," she wailed. "Maybe he'll go away again and I'll never find him."

Colin was coming down the stairs, not looking at us or anyone. Seeing him, DeeDee snatched the note out of my hand and ran over to him.

He listened to her and examined the note, but then he looked directly at me. "Where did she get this?" he asked.

"On my desk after lunch," she told him. "Oh, Colin, could you tell Peter and me how to get there?"

He was frowning, staring down at the paper in his hand. "I have an even better idea," he said. "Let me have the captain go. Wait," he added, as DeeDee began protesting. "Think about it. Captain knows Grissi. Didn't he give him to you in the first place? Captain can get there and back faster. If Grissi is there, he can bring him to you."

"But I've waited," she wailed. "I've looked and waited and I can't stand waiting any more."

He nodded again, then slipped his backpack off his shoulders. "Here," he said, handing it to her. "You feed the iron-yard cats for me while I go find Captain. I'll be back by your house for it later. Okay?"

She hesitated, then sighed. "Okay, Colin, but hurry."

Her two little friends, who had stood nearby whispering through all this, parted to make room for her. I glanced back, expecting to see Colin heading off down the street to find Captain. Instead, I saw him running up the steps to go back into the school building.

9

The Coming Storm

The wind was blowing things around the streets by the time we got home. We had winds in Peoria but they just blew. This was the kind of damp, gusty wind that went right through a down jacket like a laser beam. When we stopped off at home, DeeDee and I both put on an extra sweater before going to the iron yard.

Mr. Farley was pushing a shopping cart of groceries up the path toward the courtyard of the church as we went by. "I thought you were going to find me a church cat," he teased DeeDee. "Mrs. Joon almost missed her bus this morning telling me what a wonderful cat you found for her."

DeeDee studied him thoughtfully. "Your cat will be just as wonderful," she told him.

When we had emptied the food from Colin's knapsack into a big round circle, DeeDee and I squatted in the middle to watch the cats eat. Suddenly she caught my arm. "Where's Cream?" she asked. "Cream isn't anywhere." She patted Unk as she stepped over him to go look.

She was calling softly, searching in and around everything in that big messy yard, especially where the old things from the iron works were stacked. I yelled at her to be careful. The stuff was propped every which way and could fall on her.

She held up her hand and waved at me. Then she went over to where the cab of the old truck squatted. I saw her kneel and peer into the darkness underneath.

When she came running toward me, her eyes were round with wonder. "Three," she whispered. "Colin said it was almost time. Cream has three beautiful blind babies. It's nice and warm under there and it smells really good, too."

That didn't make the world's best sense until DeeDee showed me where to kneel to see the kittens. Cream's eyes were glowing orbs in that darkness. She was curling and uncurling her paws as she licked the tiny, sausage-shaped babies against her stomach. The protected spot she had chosen amidst the debris under the truck was almost like a cave and only a few inches from the kitchen vent of one of those downstairs restaurants I had seen so many of on the main streets.

In any case, the warm air flowing from the restaurant's rear grating was heavy with the delicious, spicy scent of Middle Eastern food.

"Peter," DeeDee said after a minute. "Something awful could happen to them there. A dog maybe, or a bad cat."

I nodded, wishing for her sake she had never met Captain, had never seen Grissi, had never taken this whole world of worry onto herself.

I quoted Colin's words: "Home is what you've got."

She came right back at me with the rest of his words. "Until the right owner comes along." She paused. "Listen, Peter," she said urgently. "Stay here with them and keep them safe. I'll be right back."

"DeeDee!" I shouted after her. It was no use. She was pelting toward the corner on those stick-skinny legs.

She was gone a long time. I watched the other cats and tried to figure out how you could draw them like that, all eating in a circle, and still keep them looking different from each other. I took a handful of food and set it back where Cream could reach it. She looked at it but didn't move toward it. Maybe she didn't want to disturb the kittens tugging at her for milk.

I didn't recognize the woman with DeeDee at first. I had never seen Huldy Zimmer except in the bookstore. She was bundled in a hooded coat and leaning against the wind.

She barely nodded at me as she followed DeeDee over to where the kittens were hidden. I could hear both Mrs. Zimmer and DeeDee talking softly to Cream. At last, Cream rose and came out to flow against DeeDee's hand. DeeDee herself lifted the kittens into the nest that Huldy

Zimmer made of her scarf. Cream began mewing pitifully when Huldy stood up with her babies.

"Maybe I could carry Cream back to the bookstore for Mrs. Zimmer?" DeeDee asked me. "It won't take a minute."

I nodded and settled back to wait, slapping my arms against the cold. As long as DeeDee was parceling out cats, she wasn't waiting at home for Captain to come with news of Grissi.

"How did you manage that?" I asked DeeDee when she finally got back.

"They were just right for each other," she said. Then, kneeling, she called to Unk. "Come on, fellow, want to be a church cat?"

"DeeDee," I wailed. "What if Mr. Farley was kidding?"

"Wait and see," she said.

I waited and I saw. DeeDee came out from the church alone. "Unk looked around in there, jumped up on Mr. Farley's highest bookcase, and went right to sleep," she told me. "It was wonderful. Now let's hurry. Maybe Captain has come."

Captain hadn't come. Instead, Mom was in the living room with a visitor. I don't know why it scared me when I realized that the man standing before our black marble fireplace was Mr. Lazarus.

He greeted me with a nod and then spoke to DeeDee. "I hate to disappoint you, DeeDee, but Grissi has not been found."

"Did Captain go to that place?" she asked, standing very stiff in the doorway.

"The note was a hoax," he said. "A mean, ugly trick that someone played on you."

I could tell how much she didn't want to believe him. She took a couple of steps and sat down in the chair just inside the door. "Did anybody go there?" she asked again in a stubborn little voice.

"Colin did," he told her. "The Captain hasn't been feeling well. It turned so bitter out that Colin went instead."

"And there wasn't any gray cat?"

"Not Grissi," he said.

A swift light of hope came in her eyes. "But there was a gray cat."

"With blue eyes," he told her.

She stood up very stiffly and said, "Thank you very much." As she started up the stairs, Mom flew after her, leaving Mr. Lazarus and me there alone.

"What's this about a hoax?" I asked.

"Colin brought me the note. He recognized the handwriting."

I was as bad as DeeDee. "Then there wasn't any gray cat."

Mr. Lazarus sighed and turned back to the fire. "There was a gray cat, but he was dead. He was blue eyed, so it wasn't Grissi. But where the note sent DeeDee was a filthy and dangerous place for a child to go. This was a mean, heartless hoax."

"Hal," I said.

When he didn't contradict me, I asked, "Why?"

He didn't answer my question directly. Instead, he sighed and said, "Peter, a school like ours can simply expel a student for bad behavior. We have that legal right. Expelling a student is easy to do *only* if you don't ask yourself what will become of the kid after he leaves you."

I didn't mean to interrupt him but I wasn't up to a lecture. "I don't care about Hal and the school. I only want to know why he tried to hurt a little kid like that."

He turned and looked at me. "Nothing in the world is as important to Hal as appearing the big shot to that little gang of kids he runs with. DeeDee is the second grader who beat him up, remember? He had to get back at her some way, and this is the way he chose."

"I guess they were waiting at that place with the dead cat," I said, kind of sick at what he was saying.

He nodded, holding my eyes. I didn't want to ask how that gray cat had died. It was bad enough to think that maybe they had looked for a gray cat and killed it, just to get back at a little kid like DeeDee. Worse than that, if it had been Grissi they found, would they have killed him just the same?

"Maybe I do want to know what the school is going to do about Hal."

"Hal's only chance is with us. He has used up all the others."

"He's got a home, a family," I protested. "Let them deal with him."

94

"How do you think he got into this shape?" Mr. Lazarus asked me.

"Then nothing is going to be done?" I was suddenly angry.

"If you mean about Hal, that kind of doing comes slowly. But as long as he is at our school, someone is working on it. The important thing was to keep DeeDee from the shock they prepared for her. Colin saw to that, when he recognized Hal's handwriting and brought the note to me."

"Colin let us think he was taking it to Captain."

Mr. Lazarus shook his head. "The captain has been in really poor health this winter, and Colin has plainly been worried about him. I haven't seen that boy smile a half a dozen times this term. In any case, it did more good for us to go."

"Us?" I asked, surprised by this.

He nodded. "You might say that Hal was a mite surprised when Colin and I came, instead of you and DeeDee. And not pleased. When I stopped off at home, I had a call from Colin. He asked if you and DeeDee would mind feeding the iron-yard cats for a few days until he can come do it again."

"Will he be at school?" I asked, thinking about his knapsack down in the hall.

He hesitated, then shook his head. "Probably not," he decided. "But I will be in touch with him for sure."

I hesitated. What did I want to say to Colin that could be carried in a message by a teacher? Then it came to me. "Tell him Cream had three kittens but DeeDee found homes for all four of them, plus Unk."

He looked at me a moment and then laughed softly. "You are either going to have to write that down or translate it."

When I explained, he nodded and crossed to the table where Mom had set his hat. "Tell your mother good-bye for me. I know Colin will appreciate all that you and DeeDee are doing."

Dad is big on weather fronts. He said the wind that was still blowing the next day would get worse before it got better. "When a bad front like this one gets stalled, it can take a long time to move on out."

Tell me about weather fronts.

DeeDee and I fed the iron-yard cats the rest of that week, because Colin didn't come back to school. Our classroom had this big hole where he usually sat. I wanted to talk to Colin, to thank him for what he had done for DeeDee. Instead the wind blew and DeeDee and I fed the cats the big bag of food that had been left when Grissi went away. All this time, DeeDee kept parceling those cats out through the neighborhood without ever getting one turned down. It was almost spooky how she did it.

The druggist and his wife took Moonshine. They lived in a little flat above their store. You could see Moonshine up in their usually sunny window almost any time of day, staring down at the street through the red blooms on a gigantic geranium plant that half filled the casement.

Mr. and Mrs. Pucci fought over whether Guinness was his cat or hers, and they offered a free bag of cat food to anyone whose cat weighed more then Guinness' twenty-two pounds.

Bumble was promised to the postman, whose name was Rick. He had to wait until Saturday afternoon to take him home. Rick said that carrying a cat in his mail pouch past the loose dogs of Brooklyn was higher adventure than he wanted to take on.

Then it was Friday, and a new storm system coming up the coast was so bad that it made the front pages of all the papers and pushed the political news to second place in the newscasts.

Colin still hadn't been back to school, and nobody had seen Grissi anywhere. DeeDee and I were on our way home when we saw Mr. Farley sweeping away the trash the wind kept blowing into that little courtyard by the church.

I waved at him, but DeeDee flew down the path to speak to him.

I figured she was sending a greeting to Unk, who, according to Mr. Farley, had become the darling of the entire Parish.

"Those of our members who are much taken by the antiquity of this fine old church revere his great age," he had explained. "The young and liberal members are proud of his battle scars, while the conservative parishioners approve of his haughtiness toward the young male cats that wander near." He had winked at us then. "Those who have no politics but God's relish the way Unk manages always to perch on the highest point in any room."

I slowed my gait, waiting for her. It was funny to remember how much I used to hate having to walk with her. Our search for Grissi had ended all that. We had walked that neighborhood too many times together even to think about it. I knew people in Brooklyn who wouldn't have given me a second look without DeeDee chattering along beside me.

I had crossed the street before she started after me. She was stumbling along blindly as if she couldn't see. Her book satchel was trailing on the sidewalk behind her. My first instinct was to yell at her about the books. Never trust your first instinct with a little sister. Instead, I turned and went back for her.

"DeeDee?" I asked, then stopped. She was crying the helpless, silent way she had that first night after Grissi was gone. There wasn't any make-believe about these tears. These were real tears, streaming from anguished eyes.

I knelt to be her height. "Kiddo," I said softly, "what's the matter?" Then I thought: "Nothing has happened to Unk?"

She shook her head and threw her arms around my neck, hanging on hard. "It's Captain," she sobbed. "Captain Jinks is dead."

10

The Breakthrough

Death is almost a media event when you are eleven. You see people die on TV and appear the next week in a different program. You see real death covered in the news, sudden distorted views of bundles on stretchers or glimpses of crumpled figures like dummies in blasted streets. Even newspaper pictures of dead people make them look as if they had always been dead.

Nobody I ever really knew had died. All the deaths in our family had been of ancient relatives whose faces I could not bring to mind.

Captain Jinks was as alive to me as DeeDee, spilling hot tears down the side of my face. Thoughts of him flashed in my mind like pictures in a videotape, too fast to see, but fast enough to register like a slap.

Captain at the bottom of our stoop. Captain's footprints in the center of that spider web of cat tracks. Captain. Captain. Captain.

"But how?" I asked. "Where? What happened?"

DeeDee loosened her grip on my neck and snuffled mightily. Then she slid her hand inside my mitten and sighed.

"Mr. Farley said his heart hadn't been working right for a long time. He was getting ready to go out feeding cats somewhere and fell down sick. His grandson found him. Oh, Peter." She began to wail again. I walked her the rest of the way home in under my arm. I rang the doorbell about eight times before I remembered that Mom had said she might be late getting home that day. I found the key in our same hiding place we had used in Peoria, and DeeDee and I went on in.

I'm not the greatest shakes in the kitchen but I can measure cocoa mix and get the right burner on by trial and error. I peeled the cellophane wrap off the cookies Mom had left out for us and put them in front of Dee-Dee.

She cupped both hands around her mug of cocoa and let it breathe hot in her face, just staring. "Peter," she said after a while. "Who's going to feed all those cats?"

That was the first time I thought of Colin. Colin had been the captain's friend. Colin quoted the captain all the time. Colin fed the iron-yard cats on weekdays, and the captain fed them on weekends.

I had never heard Colin mention his family at all. I had never seen him pal around with anyone special at school. But he and Captain were good friends. Who was sitting with him over cocoa with too much marshmallow cream in it, as I was sitting with DeeDee?

"Finish up," I told DeeDee. "Let's go feed the cats." Maybe we would see Colin. Maybe I could tell him how sorry I was to hear he had lost his friend.

"But we used the last of the cat food last night," she said.

"Then we buy some more," I told her. "I have money."

It hadn't occurred to me that everyone in the neighborhood was going to stop us to talk about the captain.

Cream was lying on a pillow in the window of the bookshop. At first glance you would have thought she was watching her kittens as they rolled and tumbled over each other. Actually she was sound asleep, with her head held up like that to fool the kittens into thinking she was awake and would keep them in line.

Mr. Zimmer was busy with a customer at the cash register. His wife, flicking a feathery duster over the card rack, saw DeeDee and me through the window and shot out the door.

"You heard about Captain, then?" she asked, seeing DeeDee's face all puffy from crying. She shook her head. "We should all just pull up stakes. It will never be the same, never the same." Then, with a wail, she went back in, letting the door bang behind her.

Cream opened her eyes dreamily and stared a moment before drifting back to sleep.

Mrs. Pucci didn't say anything when we first walked into the store. When DeeDee and I went back to the pet food shelf, she followed us.

"You found your Grissi?" she asked. She spoke carefully as if afraid her question wasn't the right one.

"Not yet," DeeDee said. "Peter and I need food for the cats that are left in the iron yard."

Mrs. Pucci's face darkened as if she hurt somewhere.

"*His* cats," she said. "Captain's cats."

She started pulling boxes and bags of cat food off the shelf and piling them in an empty cart. "Have this," she said. "And this and this. All yours. On the house."

"Wait, wait," her husband called, coming from the back in swift, short steps. "How you think these kids carry all that? You think they got a truck or something?

"Here, DeeDee," he said, handing her the large-sized box of cat food. "That is for you to carry."

"But you, sir,"—he turned to me—"you take this." When I had the ten-pound bag under my arm, he stared at me and handed me one for the other arm. "And another for balance. Yours, all yours."

"But I have money," I protested.

"I have money too," he said curtly. "I have more money from cat food by two, three times than ever before. Why is this true, you ask? Why do I sell cat food like buckwheat cakes under syrup? That one." He answered his own question, pointing at DeeDee. "Such customers you have sent me, Miss DeeDee. Mrs. Joon, and Mr. Farley down there. The Zimmers, the druggist. Even the postman. And myself, I have Guinness." He grinned, "Such a good eater, that Guinness."

"*We* have Guinness," Mrs. Pucci corrected him.

"And, listen," he went on, ignoring his wife. "When you need more for the captain's cats, you come see me. I give you all you can carry."

The three cats that were left didn't run out to meet us the way they had for Colin. Bumble saw us first. He stood up on top of that huge trash box, stretched, and lost his balance. By the time he had picked himself up, blinking, Rowdy had come running from under the truck, his tail as stiff as the mast on a ship. Sweet Pete was last, of course, peering at us nervously from behind a fire escape before finally creeping toward us, low to the ground, with his back knees bent.

I watched DeeDee make a careful circle of the food on the ground. The cats crouched down to eat it, rumbling with pleasure.

"Do you think you can find homes for these, too?" I asked her.

She nodded without taking her eyes from the cats.

"Rick the postman is coming after Bumble tomorrow," she reminded me. "And the lady with the German shepherd in the carriage house across the street wants Rowdy. The dog and Rowdy are friends already," she explained.

"What about Sweet Pete?" I asked.

"I'm working on that," she told me.

When it started getting dark, DeeDee looked at me,

puzzled. I was always the one who was in a hurry to get home before Mom started fretting.

"I kept hoping Colin might be able to make it today," I told her.

She stared at me a moment. "Colin," she repeated in a stricken tone.

I picked up the two ten-pound bags of cat food. "He'll be all right," I told her. "Your friend Colin will be all right."

I knew Mom was home from the gleam of light from her bedroom window upstairs. Since I figured she was changing out of her city clothes to start dinner, I used the key again to let us in.

Mom called out the moment we got inside the door. "About time, you bandits," she said. "I thought you must be feeding those cats, but another five minutes and I would have come looking for you."

DeeDee stood in the hall wrinkling her forehead. "Let's leave all the cat food down here," she whispered, pointing at the coat closet where I was hanging my jacket.

When I glanced at her, she went on. "Maybe we don't need to tell Mom about Captain yet?" She paused.

"I'm trying real hard not to cry," she added almost crossly, as if I should have understood without being told.

I stuck the cat food in behind all our boots and went upstairs with DeeDee. She was right. Whenever Mom heard about Captain was soon enough. She hadn't really known him anyway, and she might not understand.

Mom was in wonderful spirits. She had convinced her client that more than three patterns in her drawing room would look "busy." And she had found the most beautiful head of cauliflower she had seen since coming to Brooklyn.

She was even in a good enough mood to tease me about the dirty cocoa dishes instead of giving me a lecture. "Have you forgotten what a He-who is, Peter Gregory?" she asked, tearing the leaves off the cauliflower head and washing it under the spray.

"He-who," I repeated. Then I grinned. "You mean He-who makes dirty dishes cleans them up? Something like that?"

"Exactly like that." When she turned toward me, her smiled faded. "No sign of Grissi still?"

"No sign of Grissi," I told her, letting her think it was Grissi alone that made my face look strange. I was glad that DeeDee had gone straight upstairs to her room. Maybe that puffy look she had from crying would go away before Mom saw her.

Mom had steamed the cauliflower so that it was a perfect circle in her blue bowl. The sauce was golden, and she had sprinkled paprika on top to make it rosy. The salad was pretty ordinary, but she had fixed those breaded chicken breasts that are like big flattened eggs. When you cut into them, butter and something green spills out on your plate. They're delicious.

By the time I'd set the table, Dad had come home and called DeeDee down for dinner.

"This is a pretty fancy dinner for just a Friday night," I said as Dad took his seat.

"She's spoiling me," Dad explained. "I have a seminar in the Catskills this weekend. I'm flying out tonight and won't be back until late Sunday."

Mom and Dad talked about his meeting and about the storm that was battering its way up the eastern seaboard. DeeDee was only poking at her chicken and I wasn't even halfway through when Dad looked up suddenly.

"I guess you didn't see the late paper," he said to Mom. "The mystery is solved." He bundled his napkin by his plate. "Here, I'll let you read it for yourself."

Mostly their news isn't our news. I went on slicing the chicken breast and letting the butter run out while Mom looked at the folded newspaper. "Oh," she said in a sad tone. Then, "My goodness. Distinguished service in the Marines? What a story. We should have known."

"Should have known what?" I asked, finally coming to life.

"You remember the old man who came to tell DeeDee to look for Grissi in the iron yard?" she began.

DeeDee sat perfectly still, her eyes round and waiting.

"Captain Jinks." Mom went on reading without looking up. "It seems he was a member of a very old, wealthy family here. An eccentric, they call him."

Then she began reading out loud. "From his early days

at Groton, he was commonly called 'Captain Jinks,' a nickname that stayed with him even after he was recognized for heroic service in the United States Marine Corps, in which he rose to the rank of Lieutenant Colonel. After the war, Colonel Jinks returned to private life but not to business. He spent his remaining years and a significant fortune in charitable pursuits. He was particularly interested in the plight of homeless animals and dedicated much time and effort, as well as money, to their welfare. His only daughter died following the birth of his grandson, Colin Cramar, also a resident of Brooklyn."

"Colin," I breathed. "If he was really a colonel, why did everybody in the world call him Captain?"

Mom and Dad looked at each other. "There's an old army marching song called 'Captain Jinks,'" he explained. "It's been around a hundred years or more. When I was a kid, we all sang it. This Captain Jinks belonged to the horse marines and fed his horse on corn and beans and swung the ladies in their teens. It's a great song."

"It's easy to see how he came by the nickname, since his last name was really Jinks," Mom said. "Colin Cramar," she repeated, still looking at the paper. "Is that your friend Colin, DeeDee?"

DeeDee nodded. Then she bundled her napkin into a wad by her plate and asked in a tiny, strained voice, "May I please be excused? I need to cry."

Dad nodded as DeeDee slid out of her chair. Mom, startled, would have followed her but Dad laid his hand on her arm. "Later," he said. "Give her some time alone."

I didn't want to eat any more either, but it seemed awfully rude to leave them there with Dad's special dinner.

"That's a strange story," Dad said after a while. "It had to be difficult for that boy to have his only relative a strange old man wandering around feeding cats, dressed the way he was."

"Not for Colin," I told him. "Colin is not into putting on acts."

Mom sat frowning as if she had forgotten all about dinner. "You certainly have all kinds in that school of yours, don't you, Peter? That horrid boy that tried to play the ugly trick on DeeDee, and then this Colin."

"We sure do," I agreed, knowing where I fitted into that range.

At a signal from Dad, Mom went upstairs to comfort DeeDee. Dad refilled his own coffee cup and sat back down by me. "This Colin Cramar, is he a friend of yours, too, Peter?"

"I am a friend of his," I told him, conscious of the difference.

11

The Storm

Dad hated to leave that night. He never liked weekend meetings, even back in Peoria where we were in a familiar place with our friends all around. He would have been concerned about leaving us for the first time in this new place even if the weather had been good instead of threatening.

He and Mom visited at the door while he waited for the cab that would take him to the airport. I wasn't listening to what he was saying to Mom but, when he uses that tone with me, then I know I am getting a pep talk.

DeeDee settled in her room with paper dolls. She hardly ever plays paper dolls by herself but, when she does, she is amazing to watch. She puts all the outfits on one side and all the dolls on the other. She dresses every doll, stands each one up in a line, then dumps all their clothes on the other side and starts again.

I think she plays papers dolls the way I draw alphabets. I decide what the subject is going to be and start with A. Sometimes I pick food and draw an apple, then a banana, a celery stalk, a doughnut, and so forth until I get to the really hard letters, when I crumple up the paper and start over with a new category. I draw alphabets to keep my head from thinking about things that hurt.

DeeDee went to bed early and Mom didn't last much longer. The house got so quiet that you could hear the wind outside. I had done an alphabet that was all toys. I stopped that one at xylophone and started one of things to wear. I was only kidding myself that drawing kept my mind from Colin and Captain Jinks.

Mostly I had questions. I wondered if Colin, since he didn't have a mother, lived with the captain. If he had, who would he live with now? He had been out of school all week, but what had he been doing? Tim had gone to his aunt's funeral but he had only been gone one afternoon. Mostly I wondered what you could say to somebody like Colin so he would understand how sorry you were.

I had gotten to J in my alphabet. I drew a jacket and then looked at it again. It was like Captain's jacket, or would be if I filled the pockets full of cat food so that they hung way down. After I did that, it still looked wrong. I was drawing it straight on instead of looking down at it the way I had looked at Captain standing there at the bottom of our stoop that night.

Once I got the jacket drawn, I put him into it. There

is no way that I can possibly explain how excited I got. All my life I have been able to draw anything I could see. Now I had this picture of Captain Jinks that anyone would recognize and I had drawn it from my mind instead of my eyes.

That was a new world opened for me. I went down all those dark stairs and got milk and a piece of leftover cake and tried again. This time I took away the steps and put Captain's figure in the middle of an open space, like the iron yard. Then I drew the cats all around him, eating the way they did at that ring of food. I got Unk crouched with his battered ear showing, and Cream, deep bellied as she'd been before the kittens. Miss O, Rowdy, Pete Bumble, Moonshine, and Guinness did the same thing that Captain had done. They appeared so fully in my mind that I could get them on the paper just the way they were.

When I finished I couldn't see a thing wrong with it. There was Captain, looking up in that unsmiling way, ringed all around by those feeding cats. Mom will never know how close I came to waking her up and making her look at it.

Instead I left the night-light on while I went to sleep so that I could see my picture the first moment in case I woke in the night. I knew then that I wasn't even going to show it to Mom or DeeDee. The picture was for Colin, and he would see it first.

There was no word from Colin all day Saturday or Sunday. We did all the usual weekend things like watching cartoons and buying groceries, but we all knew we were just waiting for the storm to hit or Dad to come home, whichever happened first. By late Sunday afternoon, it was clear that the storm was winning the race.

That storm was every bit as bad as the weather forecasters predicted it would be. It never rained like that back in Illinois. This didn't look like rain at all, but more as if a river had been lifted to whip through the air past our windows. The guttering along the back of the house rattled wildly as if it were going to break free any minute. From the bottom of the drain, an arched fountain spurted out onto the garden walk.

I wondered where the pigeons were. I hoped they had sheltered somewhere so the wind howling around the house couldn't get to them.

After we ate, I brought up wood and Mom started a fire in the parlor hearth. At first the smoke billowed back into the room as if the wind whipping past the chimney didn't intend to let it come out. When the logs finally settled down to burning, I lay on the rug in front of the fireplace drawing everything I could see from that position. The chair by the library table had legs like a lion. They were hard to draw because first you had to see the whole foot as a sort of thick fan. Then each of the toes was a single round ball, joined by a flowing cone to the foot as a whole. The claws were wonderful. They were like the single hard line drawn halfway around a circle. My picture of Captain was still up there in my room, unseen by anyone.

Just knowing it was there felt warm in my mind.

Mom kept getting up and walking around and then coming back to her book again. I thought about telling her that the cabs would be off the street and the buses stopped and that was why Dad hadn't gotten home from LaGuardia where his plane was scheduled to land.

I decided not to say anything. She knew all that anyway, and talking about it couldn't make her worry any less.

DeeDee, bundled in her down robe, was tangled up into a roundness at the very end of the love seat as if something or someone were sitting there beside her. I remembered when she was really little and had imaginary playmates. She always left more room for them in the chair than she kept for herself. If her eyes had not been so sober as she stared into the flames I would have thought that she was imagining Grissi was there beside her on that padded ivory seat with the woven silvery vines embroidered all over it.

"Do you want to play a game?" I asked her.

She looked over at me, her eyes entirely too big for the size of her face. She tightened her lips a minute while she thought, then shook her head.

"Thank you very much anyway," she said, as if I were a stranger she needed to be polite to.

"I could make cocoa," Mom said, obviously pulling her mind from somewhere far away. "Or popcorn, if you would like it."

DeeDee was still looking at me and I smiled a little at her. "We're fine," I told Mom. Then, like DeeDee, I said, "Thank you very much anyway."

It struck me that even though we three were all of a family and right there in the same room, we each had our separate worlds that only overlapped in our concern about each other. I drew those three circles, realizing that mine was the best of all. In spite of my unhappiness about losing Grissi, the search for him had managed to start a new life for me there in Brooklyn. I had friends all along the street. I even liked the house now, with the bubbling pigeon voices outside my window, that vigilant red light gleaming from the top of the World Trade Center, and the pattern of shadows on my wall when my own light was out.

Most of all I had quit envying and resenting DeeDee. For gosh sakes, the kid was only seven, and she was already what Mr. Lazarus called an "effective human being." I might not always like her methods, but she managed her environment in a responsible way. She might not have solved her own problem during that search for Grissi but she had pulled all those people together and solved problems for a lot of them, including, I might add, me.

The thing that impressed me the most was that she had known when to give up. In the bathroom off the kitchen, my raincoat was probably still dripping from standing there during a late afternoon trip to the iron yard, trying to get Sweet Pete to let me catch him.

"Everybody has a cat but you," I reminded DeeDee when I finally had him bundled in the towel. "I know that Mr. and Mrs. Larson would understand if you wanted to keep him."

"I had a cat," she reminded me. "I had Grissi."

I tried to make a joke of it as we sloshed through the puddles toward home. She was hanging onto the hem of my jacket, her head bent against the rising wind.

"Mom and Dad had me and they went ahead and had you," I reminded her. "That wasn't a bad deal at all."

She looked up at me to see if I really meant it. When I grinned back, she smiled and shrugged.

The phone rang a little after nine. I have never seen legs unwind as fast as Mom's did. You could tell right away that she was talking to Dad, that his plane was down, and he was in some safe place. She came back in that bouncy way, rising a little on her toes.

"Dad said we should all go to bed," she reported, smiling. "When the cabs start running again, he'll be home, too."

12

The Shadow in the Garden

I don't know how long I had been asleep when I became conscious of the steady, frantic barking of that dark dog, Butch. I rose on my elbow and sighed. What a pest that animal was. The rain was still sweeping against the window, but the wind only slapped a little without howling. Then it dawned on me. Butch had to be outside or I wouldn't have been waked up by his barking. It was no wonder he was such a cross, unpleasant animal if nobody cared enough about him even to bring him in out of a storm like this. What good was a silly little doghouse tonight?

I might have gone back to sleep if DeeDee hadn't appeared silently by my bed. She had pulled on her robe but hadn't buttoned it, had only tied the belt tight around her middle. When I reached for the chain on my lamp, she caught my hand.

"No," she said. "Come and see."

The floor felt icy under my feet, and I dragged my robe

on to follow her to the window. I realized at once why she hadn't wanted a light. It was hard enough to see through the rain without being blinded by a reflection. The whole world out there looked freshly lacquered. Everything that was touched by one of the security lights or caught the gleam from the streetlights shone as if it had been polished. A river was running through our garden from the house toward the alley beyond. The birdbath in the Larson backyard was overflowing, and the wind caught the water as it fell and sent it flying.

I couldn't see the dog from the window, but I knew he was hurling himself against the fence again and again, the way he did when anything disturbed him. His bark had even begun to sound harsh, as if he were giving himself a sore throat.

"There," DeeDee said. "Look, on the bench."

I don't know why I had not seen it right off. Something was crouching, all round and self-contained, on the concrete bench. It didn't look like anything, really. It was more as if a shadow had fallen there, making what you knew was a straight line look curved.

That's what I told her. "It's only a shadow from something."

She shook her head. "I saw it go there. It came along the fence and crossed the yard to get there."

I whistled softly. "No wonder Butch is barking. It's got to be a cat."

She shook her head. "It can't be more than a kitten. Do you think it's safe out there?"

I turned and looked at her in the dark. "Nothing is safe out there. Do you want me to go bring it in?"

All this time that she had been getting people and cats together like a marriage broker, she had never once suggested that a cat come into our house. I couldn't believe she was suggesting it now.

She didn't answer in words but nodded, still staring down at the glistening garden.

I put my raincoat on over my pajamas. When we got all the way down to the back door, I took my slippers off and left them there. I could just imagine them curling up at the toes like the ones in the Arabian Nights if I waded outside in them. I couldn't find my hat so I grabbed a towel and wadded it on my head. DeeDee grinned that tight way she does when she isn't sure you want her to laugh at you.

It was loud out there. Everything gurgled and chimed and splatted, and all the time Butch kept up that painful alarm of his. The water was icy around my ankles. The dead leaves and sticks carried along in that tide grabbed at my feet like drowning things.

I was halfway down the garden path when the kitten turned to look at me. It was hideous. Its fur was pasted to its body like water and the pattern of its bones shone through, making it look like a mole. But its eyes, staring at me, were that same shade of yellow that Grissi's had been.

When I got close, the kitten took a flying leap off the bench and landed on the flooded path.

"Here, kitty," I called softly, holding out my hand. It didn't move but only stared at me. I knelt down and groaned to myself to feel the tail of my raincoat floating on the puddle behind me. What was done was done. "Here, kitty," I repeated, trying to coax it with my open palm.

That kitten moved so fast that I almost didn't see it go. It was off like a shot, skittering by me through the puddles toward the back door. I turned just in time to see it race past DeeDee, who was standing in the rectangle of light from the doorway.

If the little creature hadn't been dripping wet, we might have had a terrible time finding it. As it was, we followed the rainy trail right straight through the basement to the closet in the front hall. It was peering out at us with those almond-shaped yellow eyes from behind one of the boots I should have worn to the garden.

DeeDee didn't so much speak to the kitten as croon. Then she knelt down and took that dripping, boney, gray mass in the crook of her arm and carried it upstairs to the kitchen.

I warmed the milk that we gave it in Grissi's dish. DeeDee acted as if she had been in the cat-drying business all her life. First she blotted the kitten all over, then rubbed it gently with the towel. The tips of its fur were still wet and spiky when it started purring. By then, I realized that it was a little calico female—all calicos are females—and not a solid gray at all. She had splotches of lighter gray, almost a bluish color, in with the charcoal.

Around her nose she was yellow, with a touch of white.

Mom, who hadn't waked up from all our commotion with the kitten, heard Dad's key in the lock from clear upstairs. Tying her satin robe as she went, she stuck her head into the kitchen on the way down to meet Dad. "Good heavens!" she said. Then we heard only the slap of her slippers on the steps going to the basement.

Mom and Dad were arm in arm when they finally got to the kitchen door.

"Well, what's all this?" Dad asked, looking down at DeeDee there on the floor beside the wicker basket with the calico lining. "Don't tell me that the search finally succeeded."

DeeDee rose and went over to offer her face for a kiss. "Yes and no, Daddy," she told him. "We didn't find Grissi, but we found a lot of other people's cats."

"Then is this another Grissi?" he asked, peering into the basket.

She shook her head and smiled that tight little smile. "This is Smudge. I decided that Grissi needed a little sister, like Peter needed me."

Smudge. How had she come up with the perfect name so fast? And I really liked it that she had understood what I meant about having her for a sister.

Colin was back in school the next day. Nobody knew what to say to him. At least they didn't stare. Even Hal Sanders behaved himself that day, which is probably the highest tribute he can pay anyone.

Colin came up to me when I was waiting outside for DeeDee and her friends.

"Okay if I walk along home with you and the kids?" he asked. "I think you've got my backpack at your place."

"Great," I said.

Our awkward silence was broken by DeeDee's flying down the stairs. That kid is spooky. I've said so all my life and I mean it. It is almost as if she puts herself inside the other guy's head and finds what he wants the most to hear. She grabbed Colin around the waist and hugged him hard. "Oh, Colin," she said, her head still against his jacket. "I miss Captain, too. The whole world misses Captain."

He laid his hand on her head the way Dad does and looked at me with only his eyes smiling. In that moment it struck me that he was like Captain. The captain hadn't smiled either, except with his eyes. And even if Colin had been a fellow who naturally smiled a lot, he probably would have been pretty sober faced these past months. After all, he had known what we had just learned, that Captain was a very sick old man.

On the way home, Colin heard all about the cats and where they had gone and how everyone thought he had the best of the iron-yard cats.

"And wait," DeeDee told him. "Just wait until you see Grissi's little sister, Smudge."

Colin gave me another one of those warm, amused looks, and we were home.

When Mom asked him to stay for a while, he hesitated.

"I need to make a phone call first," he told Mom.

When he finished, he settled with us at the kitchen table. "That was Nellie. She's been with Captain and me ever since I was born. The three of us really got along well."

DeeDee frowned up at him. "Where will you live now?"

I saw Mom's appalled look, but Colin didn't take offense at all. Instead, he took another cookie from the plate and nodded at DeeDee.

"Nellie and I plan to stay where we are, just like before. When Captain found out how sick he was, he asked me what I wanted to do if anything happened to him." Colin hesitated just the length of a breath, before going on. "I thought about it a long time. I have cousins off in Delaware that I hardly know. What I saw of them, I didn't like. They snickered at Captain's nickname, and were ashamed of the way he dressed and went around feeding animals. Since they didn't understood Captain, they probably wouldn't understand me, either. I decided to stay here and go to the same school and live at home with Nellie until I am old enough to go off to college. Captain fixed it legally so we could do that. By then, Nellie will want to retire, too, so we'll come out even."

"Is Nellie a a part of your family?" DeeDee asked, clearly a little confused.

Colin gave me that amused look. "In the beginning, she

wasn't, DeeDee," he said. "Now she *is* my family and we both think that's the way it ought to be. Right now she's a little nervous about having the responsibility for me all by herself. That's why I needed to call."

"She'll get over that after a while," DeeDee assured him. "Like Mom did with me."

After Colin made friends with Smudge, I asked him if he would like to come up to my room. "The backpack is down in the hall," DeeDee told me.

I nodded. "Can't I ask him up to my room?"

She shrugged, took another cookie, and broke off a piece for Smudge to nibble.

The minute I started to open my door, panic hit me. What did I think I was doing? What had seemed so right that rainy night might really upset him. Maybe he wouldn't see it the way I did.

"Listen, Colin," I said. "I did this thing and thought you might want it. Now I am sure you won't." I was hanging onto that doorknob as if someone were going to force me away.

"Can't I just look and see?" he asked.

His eyes had that measuring look again.

"This isn't any act," I told him. "I just don't want to hurt you."

"I know that," he said, waiting for me to open the door.

He stood and looked at that picture of Captain and the cats for a long time while I quietly died. I could feel places inside me shriveling up from my stupidity at ever painting it, and, having painted it, at showing it to him.

When he finally turned to me, even his lips were smiling. "Peter, that's great, just great." Then he frowned and looked back at the picture.

"I thought you said you could only draw things that you could see."

"I found a new way of looking," I told him.

When he just waited for me to go on, I tried to explain. "It's as if I look inside myself and draw what I see there. It's like a breakthrough," I added, remembering how exciting it had been to find Captain there inside that circle of his cats.

"A breakthrough," he repeated, nodding. "Peter, do you think your mother could help me get it framed? I'd die if anything messed it up."

That's all he said. It was all I needed to hear. Mom leaped to the project with her usual gusto and told Colin she had found the most wonderful framer in Brooklyn only a few blocks away.

Most of the mess made by the storm was cleaned up by the time Colin took his picture of Captain home a week later. He had fallen into the habit of stopping by after school. After a couple of nights, Mom talked to Nellie on the phone and asked permission for Colin to stay for dinner.

Dad liked Colin as much as the rest of us did. After that first time, Colin had dinner with us lots of nights.

Sometimes he beat me at chess before he went on home. I had always beaten Tim, but friends are different like that.

Within a month, Smudge was as plump as Grissi had ever been and was growing so fast you could see it happen. Her face is shaped very differently from Grissi's, and when I paint her picture I have to use three separate shades of blue and gray.

All the people who had adopted the iron-yard cats gave them new names, except Rick the Postman.

"People are always asking me how Bumble, the son of Bonkers, is getting along," he explained. "It gives Bumble the class he needs."

Colin and I decided that changing the cats' names didn't matter that much. You are who you are, no matter where you live, or what you're called. And sometimes nicknames even sound affectionate. Like "Captain" had, like "Peoria Pete" does now when one of my friends yells it across the school yard. And I must say that Joons' Moon is one of the better cat names I have ever heard.

Colin and DeeDee and I all still look for Grissi down the alleys and on the garden fences wherever we go. Sometimes at night I even think I see him for a minute from the dark of my window. So far, I have only seen shadows.

But who knows?

AVON CAMELOT'S
FUN-FILLED FAVORITES BY

BARBARA PARK

"Park writes about youngsters in a way that touches reality, but makes the reader double over with laughter."

Chicago Sun-Times

SKINNYBONES
64832-6/$2.50 US/$2.95 Can
The story of a Little League player with a big league mouth.

OPERATION: DUMP THE CHUMP
63974-2/$2.50 US/$3.25 Can
Oscar's little brother is a creep, but Oscar has a plan...

DON'T MAKE ME SMILE
61994-6/$2.50 US/$2.95 Can
Charlie Hinkle has decided to live in a tree—and nothing can make him give up his fight!